THE SPELTHO

The Tale *of the* Merdogs

BOOK ONE

ASHLEY CLARK

The manufacturer's authorised representative in the EU for product safety is
Authorised Rep Compliance Ltd, 71 Lower Baggot Street, Dublin D02 P593
Ireland (www.arccompliance.com)

Troubador Publishing Ltd
Unit E2 Airfield Business Park,
Harrison Road, Market Harborough,
Leicestershire. LE16 7UL
Tel: 0116 2792299
Email: books@troubador.co.uk
Web: www.troubador.co.uk

ISBN 978-1-83628-406-2

British Library Cataloguing in Publication Data.
A catalogue record for this book is available from the British Library.

Printed and bound in Great Britain by 4edge Limited
Typeset in 11pt Minion Pro by Troubador Publishing Ltd, Leicester, UK

This book is dedicated to Cromwell, Trooper, Rafe, Hunter, Kipling and Nimrod – the original merdogs and my faithful companions.

Contents

Dramatis personae

Earl Simon Spelthorpe MC (12th Earl of Spelthorpe) b. 1890
Countess Helen Spelthorpe b. 1893
Victoria b. 1920; Edward b. 1923; George b. 1924
Black Labrador: Zulu; Siamese cat: Simba Jike

Julian Johnson (Estate Manager) b. 1881
Julia Johnson b. 1888
Joanna b. 1914; Jennifer b. 1916

Ash Cromwell MC (Deputy Estate Manager) b. 1890
Lisette Cromwell b. 1892
Michael and Lucy (Twins) b. 1920
Red Fox Labradors: Trooper, Rafe, Hunter, Kipling, and Nimrod.
Collie: Odette (Odi)
Siamese cats: Duma and Chui

Major Rufus de Lisle (Estate Veterinary Surgeon) b. 1880
Anna de Lisle b. 1885
Jeremy de Lisle (Deputy Veterinary Surgeon) b. 1911
Red Fox Labrador: Boudicca

Boynton MM (Estate Head Keeper) b. 1890
Labradors: Black and Tan

Reverend Paddy Collins MC (Vicar of Spelthorpe) b. 1880
Ruth Collins b. 1882
Irish wolfhound: Gelert.

Amrik Singh (Butler to the Spelthorpe household) b. 1883
Jasmir Singh (Estate Shop Manager) b. 1884

Foreword

The Tale of the Merdogs is a work of fiction set in the 1930s in rural Norfolk. The Spelthorpe Estate and community does not exist, but it is based on the Norfolk coastline with features from estates and locations elsewhere in England where the author has visited or worked. It is a story that is intended to take the reader back to a time that was forged in the aftermath of the First World War and how this affected the lives of those who lived and worked in a close-knit rural community that no longer exists. This also was a time of rapid technological and social change when the end of the decade was overshadowed by the threat of further conflict. The characters have been created to steer the reader through this time and to portray the loyalties, affection and love that bound such a community together.

The merdogs are based on the characters of real dogs and their relationship with the mermaid is intended provide a stimulus and magic to introduce historical events.

This is the first book in a trilogy. The second book will take Spelthorpe through some of the key events of the Second World War and how they affected and involved the lives of the characters introduced in the first book.

The third book *Spelthorpe at Peace* follows a similar pattern and will take the reader to Spelthorpe and other parts of the world in which members of the Spelthorpe family were deeply involved between 1945 and 1953.

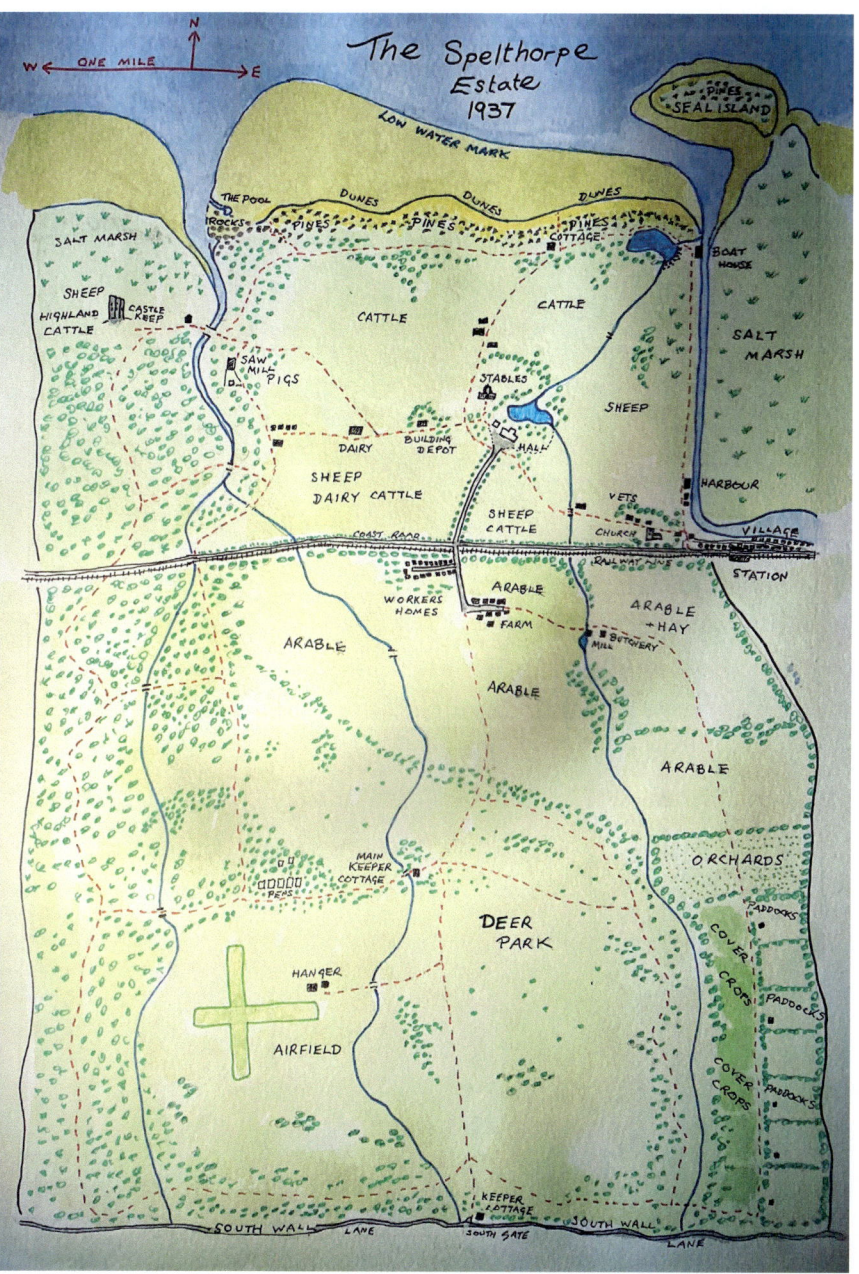

'If history were taught in the form of stories, it would never be forgotten'

Rudyard Kipling

1

The cottage by the sea

Thursday 1st September 1932

The convoy trudged along at a mere one knot. In the middle was Ash Cromwell performing his usual breaststroke and keeping a keen eye on the five escorting Red Fox Labrador dogs whilst offering words of affection and encouragement that pleased his boys. In the front were Trooper and Nimrod, strong lead dogs and to the sides Hunter and Rafe. Kipling, the fastest and most streamlined dog in the water, zig zagged around the others. They were of different ages. Trooper was the oldest and lead dog at ten. Powerful Nimrod the curious one, was the youngest at just two. Each had a unique character with different skills, but together they formed a talented team. All the dogs had learnt over the years from Ash, but importantly from each other. They were about 200 yards out from the shore. Waves were never too high here because the water was shallow – less than a fathom – and it would not support the massive waves only found in deeper water. At low tide the waters receded across the mudflats for up to half a mile.

It was a dull, damp day but the water was warm. We were in what Ash called an 'ember day'. These were the days of September to November when the night-time temperatures fell, and the nights drew in with the onset of autumn. The sky was often grey, but the sun would still punch through in patches, bathing the swimmers in a bright glow and making the gulls stand out in a brilliant white against the grey of the sky, whilst lighting up the white sand on the shore of Seal Island one mile across the bay. In early September the water was at its warmest after four months of sun. Water from the Gulf Stream was bringing the warm currents up from the Caribbean on the other side of the Atlantic. That raised the base temperature in these English waters but here things could be warmer still on afternoon tides after the morning sun had heated up the mudflats which in turn heated the water as the tide came in.

As they swam along, an occasional common seal would pop its head up and look around, then dive under the water only to resurface a hundred yards further on. Gulls would circle and the young yearlings in their mottled grey plumage would come close out of curiosity, thinking the dogs were seals, and an indicator that there were fish in the water but that was not so. There were jellyfish, but mainly the harmless common variety. These were colourless and often in large swarms. It was only the coloured variety with long trailing tentacles that could give a nasty sting, but these were few and far between. In the summer months bass would leap from the water alongside the convoy, startling the dogs as they paddled onwards.

After twenty-five minutes of swimming against the current, the convoy turned and headed back to their starting point. This was relaxation time, drifting effortlessly with the current and watching the big sky with its changing shape clouds that morphed into all types of images. They watched the dunes and pines backing the beach for any walkers or riders. The return took barely five minutes. The daily swim was a habit between the months of May and November, but with the change in tide times and the height of the tides, swim time varied. But with two tides a day there was always an option, even if that meant a dip in the dark. For the dogs this was just a normal part of the day, like a walk, but with the exception that cocking the leg was an impossibility so had to be done against the groynes on the beach. These had been placed to stop the sand from washing away. As they approached the beach a female figure appeared from the dunes. It was Lisette, Ash's wife and that could mean time for more games and competitions for the dogs. Ash asked, "How long have we got?"

She shouted back. "You will be alright for twenty minutes. It's porridge and kippers and that won't take too long."

The first game was the ball retrieve. Each dog had an allocated ball and Ash hurled them fifty yards out to sea. The dogs sat in a line and went out individually when called. It was a good game, and the dogs would only bring back their ball with a unique marking. It was exciting. Kipling had to be different. He would always spin in a circle several times before heading out to sea and set such a pace that his entire head and shoulders stood out above the water. They never failed to get their balls but in choppy conditions where they couldn't see over the waves Ash's arm signals that the dogs knew from the shooting days came in handy. The next game was the underwater retrieve, and again, Kipling excelled. Ash would lob bright white oyster shells in three to four feet of water, and they had to retrieve them. Kip was like an otter and would disappear below the surface coming up with shell after shell. The others were not so keen, but Kip was a good teacher. Slowly but surely, over the last few months they were picking up the technique that would serve them well in the days ahead. Finally, it was the test for who could bring in the biggest clump of seaweed. This was usually the brown, wrack weed with masses of bladders that made it float. Here

Rafe excelled and, like an ocean tug, he would gather several elongated clumps up to ten feet long, drag them through the water and dump them halfway up the beach to display his find to the others. It would not be wasted. Ash collected the seaweed. It would be left exposed to the rain for a couple of weeks to get rid of the salt and then chopped and composted for the vegetable garden.

"Right boys!" Ash called. The word 'right' commanded instant attention. "Back for breakfast." The dogs followed along on the short walk back to their home behind the dunes.

The gap in the pines

The cottage was set in a clearing in the pine forest about 300 yards back from the beach. There was a gap in the pines and dunes so you could just make out the roof and chimney from the beach. It was a comfortable house with four bedrooms, one of which was used as an office. There was a spacious kitchen with a newly acquired Swedish Aga cooker and stove which served as the centre of the home, and there was a large formal dining room.

Outside was a barn and two more outhouses, a greenhouse and a good-sized vegetable patch with a dozen fruit trees. There was a large pen and chicken house with a dozen hens. The chickens roamed freely in the day because the dogs saw to it that no fox dared venture anywhere nearby. The path they took snaked through the dunes along the gap and as they got close to the house a black and white border collie dashed out to greet them. This was Odette – or Odi for short – Lisette's dog, and she dashed up to Hunter and kissed him before greeting the others in turn. They all teased Hunter about his girlfriend Odi because the pair would often go off for walks in the dunes together. In fact, all the dogs had informal buddy relationships: Trooper with Rafe, Kipling with Nimrod and Hunter with Odi. Around the cottage, the dunes and the beach they had free rein and would go off to explore and patrol. Two would always stay close to the cottage and the others would return on Ash's whistle which could carry for up to a mile in any direction. Odi came swimming if Lisette wanted to swim but for the rest of the time if Lisette was on her own, Odi was usually at her side. Lisette was also mistress to two Siamese cats who were on permanent rat and mouse duty, which they relished. That, coupled with scraps from the house was all they needed. On occasions they would bring back a rabbit or an unwary pigeon, but they left the chickens alone because the hens would peck at anything that threatened them. Nimrod also avoided the chickens after receiving a peck on the nose as an over curious puppy. The cats lived in the barn because it gave them more independence, but they displayed doglike qualities, craving affection. They would sometimes come along on walks. On cold days they would come in the house and curl up with the dogs who would allow the cats to groom them.

Breakfast almost always involved porridge, which the dogs had with chunks of meat or fish thrown in. Ash and Lisette had the porridge followed with eggs, bacon or fish but never the same two days in a row. By eight breakfast was done and Lisette was off on her bicycle along with Odi. Lisette did mornings up at the big house on the estate a mile further inland where she worked as a tutor for the earl's children and helped with secretarial issues. It was less than ten minutes on the bicycle with only a gentle rise to the Hall. Odi helped with some of the lessons as a reading dog as the children liked to read to her and that helped their reading confidence. Odi was incredibly bright and knew numbers up to ten and had a vocabulary of a few hundred words in both English and French, so all this helped animate the lessons. Lisette's mother was French, and with much of her childhood spent in France she was totally bilingual. The earl had insisted that all the children spoke French, as he felt it was something that would open doors for them in later life.

Ash managed the coastal section of the estate and in the absence of the estate manager, he would stand in. The whole estate stretched for three and a half miles along the coast and four and a half miles inland. In all there were about 9,000 acres. Ash oversaw the beach, dunes, deer park and extensive woodland on the western side of the estate as well as a stretch of salt marsh used for rough grazing with 150 Romney Marsh sheep and a dozen hardy Highland cattle. About 5,000 acres in all. He also managed the three gamekeepers. On the eastern side was an inlet from the sea that went a mile inland with a harbour at the end and the village. Fishermen paid their mooring dues directly to the estate along with tenants in the village and those in the businesses and shops along the waterfront. Ash was there to troubleshoot any issues. The estate had a boathouse with a fisherman's work boat, a small twenty-foot sailing lugger, a six-berth cabin cruiser and several small leisure craft. There was a harbour master and deputy with two labourer- boatmen who also answered to Ash. On the edge of the woodland and close to the creek that separated the dunes from the marsh was a small sawmill. There were six foresters, two carpenters an apprentice, a blacksmith and an apprentice smithy employed here. They looked after the woodlands on the entire holding as well as carrying out gate and fence manufacture and iron works for the estate with some charcoal burning and traditional bodging as time allowed. Two Suffolk Punch horses were kept here in a stable with a large paddock. These magnificent, sturdy, affectionate brown beasts would drag any tree trunks out of the forest and tow the lumber cart. There was also a tractor, winches and other equipment stored in a barn. On the edge of the marsh a small cottage near the old castle keep was home to a stockman who looked after the sheep and cattle in the coastal zone.

For the agricultural remainder of the estate, there was a farm manager who dealt with the office staff, the other stockmen and shepherds, field workers, general labourers, mechanics, building and construction workers, mill, stables, dairy and shop. This meant about forty staff in addition to Ash's smaller team in the woodland and coast but overall, this was a lot less than before the Great War. Progressive mechanisation was compensating for the loss of labour. For the big house, known as Spelthorpe Hall there was a butler who managed a dozen domestic staff and two gardeners. For everyone the work was hard at times. It was all hands to the pumps at busy times like harvest and lambing and that included wives and older children, but it was a satisfying life with a real sense of community. For most there was housing provided and that included those who were no longer of an age to work full-time. The earl was kindly and benevolent to all his staff, but he found that it was repaid by their loyalty and dedication. His maxim was "You can never do enough for a good governor", and it was a model that paid off time and time again.

2

A surprise visitor

Friday 2nd September 1932

A few minutes after six found Ash, Lisette and the dogs swimming off the beach as the sun rose from the horizon in the east, scattering its golden glow across the dead calm water. It was very different from the previous day which had been a portent of the advent of autumn. Summer was trying to hold on for just a few more days. There was not a cloud in the sky. It was a sheer pleasure to be there alone totally immersed in nature and not having to share it with anything other than with what had always been. Ash and Lisette wore no costumes. There was never any need with no one about at that time of day. They had a towel each that they had left on the edge of the dunes. A couple of terns flew over and dived into the sea feeding on small fish from just below the surface. They made off when a cormorant appeared and did the same. as Lisette had joined them Odi had come along too. The collie swam well but her coat dragged, and she was not as fast as the others. Rafe and Nimrod played tug of war with the seaweed chains and as ever, Rafe was the champion at that game. These early morning tides were brilliant as they allowed a dip at both the beginning and end of the day in the best gentle light, cool and refreshing in the early morning to wake up, and warm and soothing in the early evening.

After an early breakfast Lisette took off for the Hall with Odi. The Hall was a Palladian mansion constructed in the late eighteenth century with some twelve bed and guest rooms plus additional accommodation for the domestic staff. Ash had some troubleshooting to do down at the village where some repairs were called for. He drove off with Hunter in the truck. Hunter was the best choice for this. He was an always cheerful, affectionate dog who endeared himself to all he met. That served usefully as an ice breaker if people wanted to complain about something. Hunter was a born diplomat, and Ash was wise enough to recognise that. Before leaving Ash summoned the dogs. "Right," he said, the key word that commanded instant attention. "I'm off with Hunter to the village so you lot stay. That means two on guard here and two can go off for a walk. I'll be back about midday." The dogs knew the routine and the buddy system had been drilled into them from an early age. They sat in a line but paired up as usual and watched as Ash left with Hunter in the front seat.

The dogs agreed that Nimrod and Kipling would go off for the first couple of hours. Then Trooper and Rafe would have their turn. Kipling and Nimrod dashed off through the gap in the dunes that led to the sea. There was now a gentle breeze that produced little ripples in the water, but that was all. As the tide receded quite quickly, they chased it out, dashing and splashing on the edge across the sand and mud flats as they sought out whatever the tide had decided to leave behind. It was an adventure because there was always the unexpected. Today there were lots of whelk egg cases. These were like sponges. They absorbed water but when dried out they were light and airy and would blow along in the wind. They were fun to chase and toss in the air and the dogs always liked something to chew on. The ever-watchful Nimrod spotted a seal on the edge of the water about 200 yards further along. "Let's go and check that out". Nimrod said. The dogs were familiar with the seals. Sometimes the mature seals who knew the dogs would hang around for a chat. They normally boasted about the number of the fish they had caught but they would pass on information if they had spotted anyone or anything unusual. As they got closer Kip exclaimed "That's a funny looking seal. Half of it looks like a seal or a dolphin with fish scales and the top half looks like a lady with fair hair."

The figure was face down with overlapping arms in front and appeared to be resting in the sunshine. Nimrod instinctively barked as he always did when things looked out of place. The two trotted up cautiously. The figure sat up. She was a beautiful young woman with flowing blonde hair, firm breasts and blue piercing but kind hypnotic eyes that looked deeper than the surface.

"You can pack that up Nimrod." she said. "I don't like any more noise than is necessary."

"How do you know my name?" asked Nimrod.

"I know you all Kipling, Hunter, Trooper, Rafe and Odette, and I know your master Ash and mistress Lisette and the twins Michael and Lucy. They have been away for a month. I have swum with you most days. You didn't see me because I was under the water, and I heard every word, but I never show myself when adults are around. That would spoil things. It would mean hundreds coming out looking for me, even though I'm only visible to young children and other creatures. The creatures don't talk to people and if the young children say they have seen and spoken to a mermaid their mums and dads put it down to an overactive imagination. That way us mermaids stay safe, and people leave us alone. I do see other mermaids and mermen from time to time but that gets boring because we always talk about the same things, and we do not get a chance to use our special powers. Each of us has a length of coast to look after. This stretch is mine. We do visit other places sometimes but only for short periods. We have always been about. I know that those who go to a church believe in angels. Just think of us as sea angels without wings but with our powerful tails we fly through the water. We like to do good things and help people and other creatures but in a secretive way."

"Why have you decided to make yourself known to us now and not before?" asked Kip.

"Well, I always like to watch and listen before I introduce myself. There is good and bad in all living beings. I have watched over you for many months and have discovered that you are very good swimmers. You are good kind and loyal dogs with not a hint of nastiness. I like the way you always looked after Michael and Lucy, so I thought now was a good time to get to know you better and to help you to be better swimmers. If that works out, I might use my special powers to make things more exciting for you. I know you are all very curious and always looking for new things to discover. I could help you with that. What has happened to the twins Michael and Lucy?"

Nimrod responded "They will be back soon. Every summer during the long holiday they go for a month to Normandy in France to stay with their grandparents. That way the grandparents can spend time with them, and they come back speaking French like French children. It normally takes a few days before they start talking properly in English again. Sometimes they mix their words. Odette knows what they say because Mistress talks to her in French a lot of the time."

Kip's tail was wagging "I'm very pleased we have met you," he said. "I love swimming and if you can make me do it better and more underwater that would be brilliant. I'm sure the others would like that too!"

The mermaid responded. "Nothing would please me more. I'll make merdogs of you all. It will take some time, but from what I have seen I'm sure you will make the grade."

Nimrod interjected. "Me too, but we must go back because the other two, Rafe and Trooper, must swap over with us. We normally work in pairs if the master and mistress are away. Could we send them up to meet you too? They will be here in ten minutes because they are both fast on land. What do we call you?"

"Call me Minerva," said the mermaid. "That is the name I like to use because it means wise and watchful. Be quick to send the other two. I look forward to our next meeting".

And so, Nimrod and Kipling dashed off back to the cottage where Trooper and Rafe were waiting. They were so excited that they gabbled out the words. Trooper told them to slow down a bit. They recounted their meeting with Minerva, and such was the enthusiasm that Trooper and Rafe could hardly wait, and they dashed off at speed through the gap in the dunes to meet up with the beautiful mermaid.

About an hour later Lisette returned to the cottage with Odi. She seemed in a hurry and grabbed an overnight bag that she strapped to the bicycle rack. She spoke to Odi. "Master will be back soon I'm off to the station. I'm staying in Folkestone tonight to meet the twins coming in the morning on the ferry from France. Be good. We'll be a family again tomorrow!"

With that she was off down the track for the fifteen-minute ride to the railway station. Odi ran beside her down to the village and returned within ten minutes. Trooper and Rafe returned shortly. They had met up with Minerva and were elated by the meeting. She had told them that over the weeks ahead she would teach them all to swim better both above and under the water. Odi and Hunter would be able to join in too, but she wanted to train them with just two dogs at a time as this would be easier for her. It would also adhere to their buddy routine and would not arouse any suspicion.

3

War stories

Ash and Hunter didn't need to spend too long at the village. There was an issue with a leaking roof in one of the estate-owned houses and some potholes around the port area. Ash said that he would assign it to the estate's construction team, and it would be swiftly sorted out. The team consisted of a foreman Jim, and five workers who had a good reputation for getting things done. Jim would always say "Never leave to tomorrow what you can do today because tomorrow there will be something else on the 'to do' list." Jim hated long lists. Ash called at the moored fishing boats. They had a load of freshly caught herrings. He tipped the boat captain half a crown and took a dozen large ones. That would make for an easy supper for them all. Fresh fried herrings with peas and mash were a favourite. It was better still for Ash when all washed down with a pint of cider – delicious!

Ash drove up to the big Hall on the Spelthorpe Estate – the ancestral home of the Spelthorpe family under Earl Simon. He had been the head of the family for the past seven years following the death of his father the eleventh Earl. Although he was an ancestral peer, he rarely attended the House of Lords unless issues of agriculture and defence were on the agenda. If he spoke it had to be from an informed perspective. He took the view that the House of Lords was a house of fools and kept the same opinion as President Abraham Lincoln – 'Better to remain silent and be thought a fool than to speak out and remove all doubt.'

The construction team and gardeners worked out of a yard and sheds secreted beyond the far side of the Hall and screened by woodland. The estate manager Julian Johnson (nicknamed JJ.), and office staff worked from an annexe to the side of the Hall, set back and adjacent to a walled garden. This provided comfortable living quarters for Julian, his wife Julia and their two teenage daughters Joanna and Jennifer. Ash always joked that they should call the annexe the Four J's House.

Ash called in at the maintenance yard and found Jim there alone. He shared a cup of tea with Jim and mentioned the issues in the village and port area. Hunter had a play with Jim's very energetic black and white springer spaniel Flush who went everywhere with him. The dogs knew each other well from past shoot days and from the time of the year they knew they would soon be out working again – happy days were ahead!

As Ash was leaving, he encountered Earl Simon on the front lawn with his black Labrador Zulu. "Good morning, sir," he said out loud as he always did when others were about. Although, in private, they were good mates on first-name terms and had been since their youth, but standards had to be maintained. Both were the same age and had grown up on the estate.

"Come inside Ash. I know it's early, but I feel like a small livener, and you can never do that on your own". Ash followed inside to the library and Simon poured large measures of Jameson's in fine cut crystal glasses. He only drank Irish whiskey

– smooth and triple distilled and they both sat down in leather armchairs to discuss the plans for the autumn.

Both friends went back a long way. Ash's father and mother had worked on the estate, his father as a wheelwright and carpenter, his mother in the dairy. Both were now retired and lived in a small cottage on the estate but always came out to help when required. This helped supplement pensions and it was good to meet up with former work mates. Ash went to the local school but left at fourteen. He was apprenticed on the estate as an underkeeper but as the years went by, he worked across the estate in several capacities. His organisational skills, ability and enthusiasm were noted. He was respected by the workers and by the age of twenty, he was working as a foreman overseeing work and projects across the board. In the meantime, he attended evening classes in town and joined the local St John Ambulance undertaking first aid courses. As a result, he became the first aider on the estate and some of the skills he acquired were useful with injured stock and during lambing. Earl Simon had wanted to follow in his father's footsteps with an Army career and gained a commission. After the military academy at Sandhurst, he joined the Norfolk Regiment as a subaltern in 1908. A year later he was made a lieutenant and served for a while in India and Kenya before returning home in 1912.

The eleventh earl had served as a colonel in the Boer War but after 31 years of army service he returned full time to the estate on the death of the tenth Earl in 1906. Still keen he had decided to create a territorial army company in 1910 using the men from the estate and the nearby villages. This was not unusual. A similar thing had happened on the nearby Sandringham Estate under the estate manager Captain Beck. Strings were pulled so Simon could take charge of the Spelthorpe Company as its captain in 1913. Ash joined the company in the same year and because of his leadership qualities he managed to secure a commission in the territorials as a Lieutenant after a four-month stint at the military academy. On his return he was given command of B platoon. Julian Johnson led A platoon. He had previously served in the Boer War as a lieutenant under the 11th earl, and one of the estate foremen led C platoon as a sergeant.

The Spelthorpe Company

Simon's older brother, David, had wanted to join but as the eldest son was destined to be the next earl inheriting the estate, and was expected to stay on to run the place. Food production was always important, particularly in times of war and that needed experience, sound judgement and leadership.

Alas, the peace guaranteed by having the biggest navy in the world was not to last. The nation states of Europe were bound together in treaties and agreements like mountain climbers roped together, so when one fell, they all fell. On the other side of Europe at the end of June of 1914 the assassination of the Austrian Crown Prince in a place called Sarajevo resulted in a tragedy of diplomatic miscalculation. Neutral Belgium was invaded by one million Germans and in doing so they murdered

6,000 civilians. Europe went to war. With no time to spare the territorials were rapidly mobilised. In November the Spelthorpe Company found itself south of Ypres in Belgium, holding the line in rapidly dug trenches. It was only the supreme accuracy and rate of fire from the trusty Lee Enfield rifle that kept the Hun at bay. Accuracy in shooting following the lessons of the South African War had always been a mainstay of military training.

Simon and Ash went out trench raiding at night, leading small groups of men through gaps in the wire with faces blacked up, armed with clubs and Webley revolvers to hit the enemy with jam-tin bombs, spreading terror and taking prisoners. It was bloody and living on the edge, but better than hanging around waiting for a shell or a sniper's bullet with your name on it. Trench warfare could be monotonous at times: cold and wet, knee-deep in mud, with irregular meals and having to cope with snipers and enemy hate in the form of shellfire. At least the raids broke the tedium of stalemate. The men stayed alert, aggressive and felt they were doing something positive. That was what the Generals wanted. For their initiative and daredevil courage in trench raiding five of the Spelthorpe Company got mentioned in army dispatches and that included Simon and Ash. Christmas came and contrary to initial expectations the war was far from over. Barbed wire and the machine gun had created an impasse with no way of punching through. The following year would demonstrate that. In parts of the front there had been a temporary truce with exchanges of gifts, a kick about with a football, sing songs and a chance to bury the dead. The Generals frowned on it asking how one could drink with a man one day and kill him the next. The fact that between Christmas Day and Boxing Day over 200 British soldiers were killed in France and Belgium made something of a mockery of any notion of truce.

In the new year hatred of the Hun increased as the propaganda machines on both sides went into action. At Easter a story circulated that a Canadian soldier had been crucified by the Germans. Then, a few days later the Germans attacked at Ypres in Belgium and used chlorine poison gas for the first time. Men drowned in their own bodily fluids produced by the burning in their lungs. In early May the company was attached to the Northamptonshire Regiment to make up for losses and in readiness for an attack to capture a place called Aubers Ridge. The trench line extended southwest of a village called Neuve Chappelle. On the eighth of May news arrived that a German U-boat had sunk a passenger liner, the *Lusitania*, off Ireland killing more than 1,000 civilian passengers.

The attack on Aubers Ridge was due the next day. The company assembled in the front trench at 0400 hours to go in as the first wave. The men were nervous and fearful of the unknown but confident in their own abilities. Captain Simon was dedicated to them all. They were his boys. He walked up the line addressing the men and quoting from Shakespeare's Henry V. "*We few, we happy few, we band of brothers. For he today who sheds his blood with me shall be my brother.*"

At 0500 hours the bombardment opened pounding the German front line 500 yards ahead. Gaps had been cut in the wire in front of the British trench. Shell after shell burst on the enemy trenches and above spraying lead shrapnel balls. How could anything survive that? The noise was deafening. Smoke and the smell of cordite were all around. Then after forty minutes the shellfire stopped briefly, and the fire moved on to the German support and reserve trenches further back. "Fix bayonets!" was the command. This was real, not training. Men fumbled with the bayonets and Ash walked up the line helping the men, patting them on the shoulder. Some vomited. Then came the whistle and the men climbed the ladders and walked forward through the shell hole-ridden landscape. After 200 yards the rat tat tat of enemy machine guns started up coming from forward to the left and right a long way off. Men started dropping. There was no stopping for the wounded. Simon broke the rules and issued the order to charge. He felt the quicker they got to the German line the less time they would be exposed. The smoke helped conceal them but as they ran forward more men fell. Men took what shelter they could in shell holes with some dodging in and out of the holes to go forward whenever the machine guns were briefly silent. The first men got to the enemy wire which was still largely intact despite the shelling. The front of the Hun trenches appeared reinforced. Captain Simon was at the wire struggling through and as they got to that point, they had passed the zone where the enemy enfilade fire had been cutting them down. German heads and rifles appeared above the parapet. Men sheltering in the shell holes fired at them and the heads ducked down. Simon was tangled in the wire and a shot struck his left forearm. He had twisted his ankle and couldn't move. He had dropped his Webley revolver but was half hanging on the wire as he waited for the inevitable. This was not right. It couldn't, it must not happen! Ash ran forward the twenty yards from the shell hole with a set of wire cutters he had taken from one of the men. He shouted back to his men "Covering fire!" and in seconds was next to Simon cutting the wire to release him. Just as he cut the final strand and put his left arm around Simon to support him back, three Germans with bayonets fixed appeared over the trench top. They were either intent on taking two officers as prisoners or more likely killing them both. But there was no time for conjecture. Simon saw them and instinctively drew his Webley. This was a man-stopper with a large .455 calibre bullet. After years on the estate, shooting was second nature, and he'd had a lot of practice with the Webley. In an instant the closest

Hun was down, then another and another, all with shots to the centre of the body at ten yards. They had not been expecting that. Ash took out one of the newly issued experimental Mills bombs from his pocket. He pulled the pin and lobbed it back into the German trench. Seven seconds later it blew, giving Ash the time to get Simon back to a larger shell hole some 50 yards back from the German line. They took cover with two other Spelthorpians. It was stalemate. The attack had failed, but to leave the safety of the hole in broad daylight would be suicide. The cries and moans of wounded men all around made for painful listening. Ash felt he had to do something. Fires caused by the shelling produced periodic smoke clouds and three times Ash went out into the smoke to bring back wounded men: the underkeeper with a broken leg shattered below the knee, one of the stockmen with a bullet in the belly and one of the gardeners with a head wound. He patched them all up with dressings and splinted the fractures with whatever was available to immobilise them and gave the men water. He was helped by one of the Northamptons. He was a lad of nineteen called Harry who had a shrapnel wound to his left hand. Ash patched him up. Harry had only come out a month earlier to join his eldest brother who was a sergeant in the same battalion. Unfortunately, when he arrived, he learnt that his brother had been lost in an attack a few days earlier. They got extra water from the canteens of the dead and more dressings too. Darkness fell some fourteen hours later. They dirtied their faces and anything that was pale with mud, and on the way back, they found a stretcher lying beside a dead bearer that was needed for the leg case. Through the night, and it took them all the night, they got them back.

All survived other than the stockman with the bullet in the gut who lasted a week. Abdominal wounds were notoriously difficult to treat because of infection. The western front was fighting in a farmyard with muck and horse dung all over.

Bullets and shrapnel would take in muddied uniform fragments deep into the wound.

The Battle of Aubers Ridge meant the end of the Spelthorpe Company. Nineteen were killed, forty-five were wounded of which thirty-two had copped a 'blighty' putting them out of the war permanently. Those left were used to make up losses in other regiments. Some 3,500 men on the British side died that day including hundreds of brave men from India who had volunteered to fight in a war some 6,000 miles from their homeland. A village in Sussex, Wadhurst lost twenty-five men on that field. In the aftermath periodic shelling went on as it did across the whole front, indeed it was shelling that killed six out of ten of those killed throughout the war. Two days later a shell burst in the British sector.

Ash was just in the wrong place at the wrong time and sustained a shrapnel wound to his left shoulder. Fortunately, it missed any vital parts, but he spent four weeks in hospital in England and another month of convalescence back in Spelthorpe. The action on that fateful day did not go unnoticed. For their leadership, example and courage under fire both Simon and Ash were awarded the Military Cross and six other Spelthorpians including Julian Johnson were recognised with mentions in dispatches.

For Simon, his war was over. The bones and flesh of the lower left arm repaired but he was left with a permanent weakness and slight deformity compared to the right. He returned to Norfolk but at least his wife of two years was pleased to have him back and that full functionality was only marginally affected. This meant a major change. The brothers swapped roles. Simon took on the running of the estate and his older brother signed up gaining a commission. After a few months as a lieutenant in the Norfolks he managed to get a transfer to the Machine Gun Corps because he found out early in 1916 that they would be using the new land ships or tanks as they came to be known. His view was that these would help to win the war and break the stalemate, and he wanted to be part of that. On the fifteenth of September he took part in the first tank attack on the Somme, the same day that the Prime Minister's son, Raymond Asquith was killed. In 1917 he was promoted to captain but alas, at Cambrai in November as his tank and 400 others advanced with spectacular success, his tank took a direct hit from shellfire, and he was killed. Whilst in England for the first time the church bells rang at the news of the initial resounding success, at Spelthorpe the only chime was the funeral bell. All at Spelthorpe were devastated. This tragedy changed things permanently and meant that Simon would inherit the estate. He did so in 1925 on the death of his father – the eleventh earl.

Ash was deeply affected by Aubers Ridge and what followed. The shortage of shells and the right type of shells needed to smash the enemy trench lines caused a national scandal. Ash was unhappy with the poor way in which casualties were treated and evacuated. He felt that better organisation was needed to free up the army doctors to deal with the casualties and given his background and extensive first aid training he asked to be transferred to the Royal Army Medical Corps which was rapidly expanding. Given his Military Cross and work on trench raiding there was no question that he was seeking an easy life. There was an urgent need for improvements in dealing with casualties. Stretcher bearers were the bravest of the brave as they went over the top not just once, but dozens of times engaged in no man's land seeking out and bringing back the wounded. His transfer was achieved early in 1916 and following further training and examinations in which he excelled he was promoted to the rank of captain. He was assigned to a support and logistical role within the Corps. On leave he returned to Norfolk and the relationship with Simon turned into a solid friendship. A relationship as a brother in arms was the strongest ever, and that applied throughout the estate with those who served and those who had lost. After the war he returned to the estate on a full-time basis and was appointed to his current role.

Simon and Ash went through the current business on the estate for an hour with another whiskey.

Simon asked, "How are the twins?"

Ash responded, "From reports I think they are doing well and as Lisette has probably told you they are coming back from their grandparents in France where they have been for the last month polishing up their French. Lisette has just gone off to Folkestone on the train to bring them back so by tomorrow we will be back to normal with school starting again on Tuesday."

Simon and his wife were godparents to Michael and Lucy just as Ash and Lisette were godparents to Simon and Helen's children Edward, George and Victoria. Victoria was the same age as the twins and Edward and George were three and four years younger respectively. All the children went to a first-class public and preparatory school some ten miles away, boarding in the week and coming home on Saturday afternoon for the rest of the weekend. Simon arranged for the estate to pay the school fees as he did for Julian Johnson's two daughters. His justification was that he wanted his managers to be available at all times and that should not be compromised by childcare issues in the working part of the week.

Ash took his leave and found Hunter out on the from lawn playing ball with Zulu – Simon's black Labrador and Edward and George. On Ash's command Hunter jumped straight back in the truck and off they went back to the cottage.

On getting back to the cottage Hunter jumped out and joined the other dogs where he learnt from them of the events of the morning.

Hunter said, "A good story but I'm not that daft!"

Trooper responded "We are not making this up. You'll find out for yourself when the master goes to pick up the twins tomorrow. We will all go and meet up with Minerva then." Ash made himself a sandwich then drove off for a quick visit to the foresters at the sawmill over on the western side of the estate.

4

The return of the twins

Lisette lodged her bicycle at the station and caught the lunchtime train to King's Lynn. There were only four trains each way every day from this small branch line. It was mainly used for freight to supply the villages along the route and to take out agricultural produce and fish. A single coach with thirty seats was ample for most days but at holiday times another larger coach would be added with a total of six trains each way between 7 am and 7 pm. Service on the London North Eastern Railway was usually reliable. An hour later she arrived at King's Lynn then took the express to London arriving at 3 pm. Lisette knew London well, having lived and worked there in her late teens. She was a confident and very attractive woman, and although her French accent had never totally left her, it was part of her charm and attractiveness. London for Lisette was just somewhere to get through, but it held no real pleasure. At heart she was now a country lady. The hustle and bustle of the city, the noise, the smells and dirt were not something she was prepared to tolerate for longer than was necessary. She found the tube claustrophobic and where possible preferred to walk if time allowed for that. From

Liverpool Street she took the tube to Victoria and onwards by train to Folkestone arriving at 6.30 pm.

Lisette was born in Paris in 1892. Her father had been working for the British Diplomatic Service in Paris since 1885 and had met her mother who was working as a teacher. They had met in the Jardin des Tuileries during the long daily lunch break that was a well-established French custom. It was the start of a whirlwind romance with marriage just two years later.

This had been an exciting time to be in Paris – the Belle Epoque as it was known. It was amazing how quickly France had recovered from the defeat of the Franco-Prussian war in 1870 and the subsequent siege when the starving population in Paris had eaten cats and dogs and the entire Paris Zoo only to be followed by the bloody suppression of the French Commune when thousands of French men and women were slaughtered by their fellow Frenchmen in the military. The rebels had become infected with that French revolutionary custom of taking to the barricades but on this occasion, it sadly failed them. The repression had been bloody and ruthless. All that was now over apart from the guilt and the need to atone.

1889 saw the advent of the World Fair and the Eiffel Tower as its centrepiece to highlight French achievements in engineering, lighting, and the arts. France led the world in new technology like the motor car. Aviation was to follow. It had been an exciting time and a busy time on the diplomatic front with Anglo French territorial disputes in East Africa but all that changed when Edward VII came to the throne of Britain as king and emperor of India in 1901. He was a great lover of France and the good things in life like cigars, fine wines and brandy but most of all French ladies, to the displeasure of his queen but she never seemed to complain. His notoriety was such that he was known not as Edward the Confessor but as Edward the Caresser who sowed enough wild oats in Paris to feed Europe. An official visit in 1904 went down so well with the population of France that a new Entente Cordiale or friendly understanding came into being between Britain and France. No doubt this was partly because of Edward's apparent naughtiness, a quality understood by the French people who until 1899 had a president with a similar reputation who used his desk for more than just the paperwork.

Lisette went to the French school where her mother taught, and French became her first language. In 1906 the family moved to Biarritz as Lisette's father had been posted there because Edward VII spent so much time in the resort. He even demanded that his ministers travel there to conduct business. After two years at France's leading seaside town for the well-to-do, Lisette's father was posted back to London where his expertise gained over the last twenty-three years was in demand. Lisette continued with her studies in London then took a job as a teaching assistant at a private school in 1911 where she remained until 1916.

Following her arrival at the Folkestone Central railway station Lissette took a short walk up to the Leas on the Folkestone cliff top where she had a hotel room booked for the night. She knew the area well having spent the early part of 1916 training there. In England hatred of the Hun accelerated throughout 1915 with the start of the 'Baby Killer' Zeppelin Raids on the East Coast. London came next. In October a British nurse, Edith Cavell working in Belgium was executed by a German firing squad. Lisette felt that she had to do something so she volunteered for the FANY- officially the First Aid Nursing Yeomanry – founded eight years earlier with the splendidly noble notion that skilled women horse riders would ride out across the battlefield administering first aid and rescuing soldiers. Lisette had learnt to ride from an early age in France. Unfortunately, the realities of the new warfare made this impossible as it was soon discovered that the horse and the machine gun did not go together well. The FANY selected young women from a middle-class background. After some initial setbacks where the British Army refused ladies at or near the battlefield it was noticed that the French and Belgians were pleased these feisty ladies could drive ambulances, so this, along with nursing and secretarial support became their main role. They had proved themselves and there was a change of mind at the War Office, so the British Army took them under their wing although as volunteers they maintained a good degree of independence.

Lisette walked along the Leas for an early evening stroll. It was very different from 1917 when the town had been packed with soldiers heading for France and thousands of Canadians were housed in and around the town and the Shorncliffe Military Camp. Hundreds of Women's Army Auxiliary Corps had also been undergoing training at the nearby Metropole Hotel. The local 'Ladies of the Night' had carried out a brisk trade with the Canadians and so much so that a nearby TB sanatorium at Etchinghiill five miles out had to be used as hospital to treat what was euphemistically called 'Cupid's Measles'. The Canadians were very, very friendly but the training regime restricted any excursions into town and Lisette was often reminded of the other explanation of the acronym FANY – "Flirt And Never Yield". She carried out some 'on the job' nursing and ambulance training at the Shorncliffe camp before heading across the channel and out to the hospital and training ground at Etaples on the French coast in June 1917. But by then she had witnessed the horror of war first-hand when on the twenty-fifth of May and in broad daylight German Gotha bombers, who had failed to reach London turned around and dropped their bombs along the route from Ashford to Folkestone. It was so unexpected. Lisette had been driving an ambulance near the harbour when a bomb dropped on nearby Tontine Street. There was a big queue outside Stokes the greengrocers. They had gathered on hearing that a consignment of potatoes had arrived. The front of the shop took a direct hit killing forty-four people instantly. Lisette drove up. It was carnage with bodies everywhere, with blood and glass. Babies were crying in their prams and horses lying in the street cut to pieces. Many victims were young children. Amidst the screams Lisette did the best she could to organise a sort of triage so those with a chance were treated and evacuated as quickly as possible. Wearing a uniform with a Red Cross armband, everyone came to her clinging on and pleading for help. Lisette endured the agony and guilt of not being able to treat them all, but her training and discipline of the last few months took over. She got her ambulance loaded and took off to the hospital. Of those taken away seventeen died in hospital. Lisette had wept herself to sleep that evening.

Lisette had a light meal at the hotel on the Leas and retired. Travelling was always tiring. She had missed the children but the opportunity for them to spend time with their grandparents and to experience and learn French with total immersion was not to be missed. She slept well and after breakfast, she walked along the Leas, past the war memorial and down the steep road that led to the harbour. This road had since been renamed the Road of Remembrance. It was the road the soldiers took to go off to France and for many it would be their last time on English soil. Soldiers went out from Folkestone, but the wounded were landed at the port of Dover in order that those going out didn't see the consequences of war, so morale was maintained, albeit briefly. As she walked into the dock area the memories of the

Gotha Raid all came back. That bombing changed history because later that year, King George changed the royal family name from Saxe-Coburg- Gotha to Windsor.

The ferry was due in at 10 am. Lisette arrived about half an hour before in eager anticipation and from the arrivals hall could make out the ferry about three miles offshore. She sat and reflected on how back in 1917, at the age of twenty-five she had left Folkestone and by the end of the day found herself at Étaples or 'Eat Apples' as the Tommies called it. The town – originally a medium sized fishing port had been transformed with a dozen or so field hospitals capable of taking up to 20,000 casualties. It was chaotic with the inevitable dirt and untidiness born from urgency. There was little room for the niceties. To make matters worse, the morale of the troops was bad because of the infamous Bull Ring training ground set in the Étaples coastal dunes. There, troops from the front and new recruits were bullied mercilessly by corporals and sergeants known as 'canaries' because of their yellow armbands. Few of the canaries had seen the front and this bred resentment which resulted in mass disorder and disobedience for a few days in September 1917. Fortunately, Lisette missed much of this as she spent most of her time driving an ambulance backwards and forwards from the casualty clearing stations behind the Somme area. Roads were always busy with supplies going up to the line and local French traffic around the city of Amiens. In fact, the city was so busy with war traffic that it was known as Camionville to the French (Lorry town). Lisette's fluent command of the French language coupled with a few choice words known only to the French combined with her natural charm and looks to helped her get through the jams at a rapid pace as she found out about shortcuts from the locals. Her ability did not go unnoticed by a handsome Royal Army Medical Corps captain charged with sorting out the mess on evacuation routes. He asked that she be attached to his unit and the FANY could hardly refuse the request of a decorated British officer. From the start, they struck it off, and in a matter of weeks they became lovers. Discretion was the order of the day, but they did manage to get some local leave with the dates curiously coinciding. They managed to get passes to Paris and spent three wonderful days together in a Montmartre Hotel in the artists' quarter with a balcony overlooking the Eiffel Tower. On the banks of the Seine at sunset and next to the imposing Beaux-Arts style Pont Alexander III, he proposed. It was an instant "Yes", but the engagement ring had to wait. They duly returned to Étaples and although military necessity meant periods of separation, only three weeks after the signing of the Armistice they were married in Paris. Three months later after resigning his commission the couple returned to Spelthorpe. The rest was history.

Lisette spotted the twins as they joined the queue for the passport check. As with all unaccompanied minors the official studied the passports carefully and asked questions. Lisette approached the barrier.

"Are these yours?" the official asked as he turned to Lisette on seeing the excitement in their faces.

"Indeed, they are," said Lisette. That convinced the officer, and he waved them through.

They dashed up. Lisette stretched out her arms and cried out "Salut. mes enfants!" and barely a second later they fused in an almighty hug, all dropping their bags to the ground.

Lisette asked "Vous avez passé un bon sejour avec papi et mamie?"

Michael instantly piped up "O! oui. C'était superbe. Nous sommes allés à Paris pour trois jours"

Then Lucy added: "On a monté le tour Eiffel jusqu'au

sommet puis Versailles, un restaurant formidable à Montmartre. Nous avons tout vu."

It was then that Michael got to the important bit, "Tout va bien avec les chiens?"

Lisette responded. "Bien sur. Ils nagent quotidiennement. Mais vous devez commencer à parler en Anglais encore, au moins après notre arrivée à King's Lynn. Papa sera là pour nous rencontrer".

They grabbed their bags and walked onto the platform for the London train. Thirty minutes later they were heading for London and arrived just after 1 pm. It was fortunate that all were travelling light. After arriving at Victoria, they made their way on the tube to Oxford Street and Selfridges. Lisette wanted a couple of things that were hard to come by up in Norfolk and she decided to treat them to new swimming costumes. Bodily changes with the twins were becoming more evident so modesty dictated more of a cover-up. She bought each a costume in fine weave navy blue wool at a modest price. With impending growth spurts she thought it unwise to buy anything more expensive, but she treated herself to the latest Lastex fabric that moulded to the body without the sagging associated with wool. It was considerably more expensive, but she felt that Ash would appreciate the visual change even if he was not going to part with the light canvas shorts that he wore for everything.

Then it was back on the tube and across to Liverpool Street to catch the 5 pm train up to King's Lynn. They managed to get a table in the restaurant car which was good because with all the rushing around they were famished. For the whole time they hardly stopped talking other than to chew their food. Tales were told of their month in Normandy on the coast where Lisette's parents had opted to live following her father's retirement from the Diplomatic Corps. It was somewhere they knew well with an annual family visit for the last ten years, but for the last two, the twins had gone on their own on the boat to be met at each end. During that time, they became known to the locals and had made friends with the village kids. They struggled to talk in English again but the main subject they always returned to was the dogs who were like brothers and a sister to them as they had grown up. In two days' time they knew they would be back on the weekly board at school and they were determined to make the most of their last two days of the long holiday break. Both were very confident with a richness of experience and conversation with all sorts of people they had met. That had given them a wisdom more advanced than their years. Michael was athletic, a little stern at times and dark, mirroring his father. Lucy was affectionate, blonde and slim and was turning into a real beauty who would turn heads in the years to come although at the present time after a month in the sun they were deeply tanned with no shortage of vitamin D in their system.

At 7.30 pm the train pulled into King's Lynn station.

5

Lessons with Minerva

Saturday 3rd September

Early on Saturday Ash took all the dogs for a quick swim. They could tell from his mood that he was going to have a busy day. He gave the dogs Winalot biscuit with chunks of venison meat from a deer that had been struck on the road by a vehicle the previous day. It had been wounded and the underkeeper had put it out of its misery. Nothing went to waste. Fallen beasts were shared out by the dog owners on the estate if there was no suspicion of disease. A haunch had been left at cottage with a note. Fifteen pounds of lean meat would feed the dogs for several days and some would be stewed up for them and the family with carrots, potatoes and cabbage. The dogs lived well. Ash firmly believed that good food with a varied diet and exercise was the key to keeping dogs at their best and he applied the same doctrine to his family.

For himself, he had porridge with thick bacon cut from half a flitch kept in the larder and two fried eggs with a mug of tea. He grabbed a couple of apples. That would keep him going all day. He fed and released the chickens and was off in the truck.

"I'm off to the sawmill," he said to the dogs. " We have a lot of cutting and dipping to do for urgent fencing, so I won't be back till late. You lot are in charge and remember – two here at all times!"

The dogs were excited but waited for a couple of hours. Time was on their side. They knew that exercise after a meal could make them ill and remembered a few years back a dog on the shoot had worked too hard after a meal and died from what the keeper said was a bloat. It got twisted up inside and when they got to the vet it was too late.

They agreed that Hunter and Odi would go off to find and meet Minerva for the first time and Kip and Nimrod would go with them leaving the senior pair behind on guard.

They walked off through the gap in the dunes that were covered in marram grass that matted the sand together and stopped it shifting. When they got to the sea's edge they trotted along. There was nobody about. Nimrod stood and let out a powerful bark. That should let her know that we are about, he thought. They walked slowly on the shore in a westerly direction. Suddenly there was a voice behind them from the edge of the surf.

"Good morning dogs! So, you have come to see me again. I've been watching and waiting, and I saw you all earlier, but you didn't spot me because I was underneath you. And who have we here?"

Odi and Hunter introduced themselves, and she answered their questions.

"Right," she said in the same tone as Ash because she knew that would get their instant attention.

"We will do an hour's practice at my special pool. It's a bit further along in the sand and rock zone but it is quite deep and clear. I can teach you there and when all of you have mastered the underwater bit, I will apply my special skills, and I will take you on adventures. When we have done the first session you can go back and send the other two and I'll train them. Are you all happy with that?"

The dogs nodded in agreement, and they went on for ten minutes up to the rocky zone. There was a natural channel from the sea with a pool about twelve feet deep in the centre. It was about five yards across and almost seven yards long in an oval shape. Minerva dropped an oyster shell about four feet down.

"Kip," she said. "Fetch that. Show them how it's done."

Kip was on to it in a flash, disappearing for less than five seconds then coming up with the shell in his mouth.

"Now if Kip can do it so can the rest of you. You must dive like a duck. Head straight down. Keep your eyes open so you can see where you are going. It will be blurred at first, but I can correct that. Use your powerful front legs to paddle down and wriggle your tail end and you will get down there. And finally hold your breath. If you are pointing down, you can open your mouth but don't open on the way up!"

And so, the dogs took it in turns. Kip always went first to show them it was possible and gradually they all got there. After a quarter of an hour, they could all manage the four foot depth. Odi found it a little harder because of her coat but as she went down it flattened with the pressure, and she gained confidence.

Minerva then dropped the shell in six feet of water. Kip succeeded first time. The others took a bit longer. Kip said, "You have seen the otters up at the creek. The only difference is they have shorter legs and webbed feet. If they can do it, we can do it".

At this point Minerva intervened, "I will help you now. As Labradors you have partially webbed feet already. I will increase the web size for you using my powers."

The dogs were very pleased with their larger front paddles. Visually there was no difference unless the paws were splayed, but in the water, things were much easier. Minerva increased the depth to eight feet and with some effort they all managed it.

"You have all done well but you are getting tired. You will be able to stay down longer if you take three or four deep breaths before you dive so I want you to practise that on your own. After all that effort I think it best you all go back for some well-earned rest and to change over with the other two. Kip can stay here with me so he can show them what to do when they get here. I'll see you all next week. Just come out when you are free, and I will find you. I am pleased. You are well on your way to becoming merdogs."

With that they all thanked Minerva and Hunter even stepped up and gave her a quick kiss. Then off they trotted with a spring in their step, pleased with what they had achieved. In ten minutes, they were back at the cottage allowing Trooper and Rafe to set off for their lesson.

Ash came back just after 4 pm. He was filthy with sweat and sawdust. The dogs were all lying dozing under the oak tree close to the front of the house.

"What have you been up to?" Ash asked "You look all worn out to me. By the look of it you have all been in the sea again." He went inside and came out with a bar of coal tar soap and a towel. "It's about time we all had a bit of fresh water."

He led them off for about a quarter of a mile eastwards to the lake filled by the stream that drained off the eastern side of the estate. It was effectively dammed by the dunes but leached away slowly. At that time it was about 300 yards long and 150 yards wide, surrounded by reeds in the shallows with willows and alders along the banks. There were ducks, and moorhens and a pair of swans on the other side. The depth varied with rainfall and season but at present it was about fifteen feet at the centre.

Ash stripped naked then went in up to his waist and

splashed all over. There were some quite large carp in the lake and some trout that kept taking flies from the surface. Ash often joked that if he kept going in naked, he might lose a vital part of his anatomy but that never stopped him. Fortunately, in that respect there were no pike. He came out and soaped up before going back in and submerging totally. The dogs went in too and Ash could not help but notice that they kept duck-diving and coming back up after a few seconds. Only Kip had done this before on a regular basis but now they were all at it. "Who taught you that?" he asked. "Have you met up with a mermaid while I was away?" He laughed out loud.

After 10 minutes he was out and walking back to the cottage with the towel around his middle.

He shouted to Odi, "Chick, chick!" and with that, she ran about the cottage and rounded up all the chickens driving them into the fox-proof pen. It was her daily job, and she excelled, staring them out and taking no nonsense. In fact, it was so easy now because as soon as the hens saw she was on the warpath, they instantly made for the pen.

Ash changed his clothes and then donned an apron. He chopped all the remainder of the venison with a load of vegetables and tossed it into a large pan that he placed on the Aga. He put in a large spoon of Bovril but remembered not to add any onions because they could harm the dogs. He boiled it, then let it simmer for an hour before putting it aside to cool. Ash looked at his wristwatch. It was 6 pm and time to go so he headed for the barn and jumped in the Morris Oxford Six. He had recently bought it new. After running it in it had proved to be both comfortable and reliable. It was ideal for family outings. At this time of year starting was rarely an issue and keeping it under cover paid off.

As he drove off, he shouted to the dogs. "Stay here. Should

be back just as it gets dark." And with that he was off to King's Lynn. After all the day's exertion the dogs were too worn out to wander of, and they could smell the cooling stew from the kitchen, so they went back to dozing under the great oak.

Ash returned as expected with the full family. As the kids got out of the Morris the dogs bounded up and their excitement was impossible to control. Michael and Lucy were part of their pack, and this had been so as the pack had grown over the years. Their bond was such that each could pick up those hidden signs and expressions shared uniquely between siblings. When the excitement had died down, they all went inside. The dogs got their ration of the stew with biscuit, and it smelt so good that Ash who hadn't eaten since breakfast had a portion too with a lump of bread and a bottle of Newcastle Brown Ale – his favourite tipple. The family had the luxury of one of the new electric fridges although most food was kept in the cool of the larder on the cooler north side of the house. As always, the dogs were fed individually in age order. That kept the discipline of the pack and Ash had found that it was the quickest way to teach each dog his name. Although Odi as a lady, always went first.

The twins were tired after the long journey. They had eaten on the train with a lot of chatter so in less than an hour they were in bed with a promise of a swim early in the morning. This was to be followed by church, a matter that was de rigueur for all senior staff on the estate. Ash had something planned for the Sunday afternoon after a quick lunch particularly as on Monday the morning would be spent on an 'all hands' job on the farm followed by preparation and return to school. The dogs went outside and slept under the oak as it was a warm evening. Ash put a record on the gramophone and poured out two small glasses of Jameson's. He and Lisette cuddled up on the sofa to the sound of Vaughan Williams's '*The Lark Ascending*', then they, too, retired to bed.

6

God's acre

Sunday 4th September 1932

The sun rose in the east, sending a warm orange glow across the lake. It was dead calm with not even the slightest ripple. There was a low cloud of mist a few feet above the surface on the southern side where swans and geese drifted in and out of visibility. The peaceful idyll was suddenly shattered as Michael, then Lucy ran and dived from the springboard only to be followed by the six dogs and finally Lisette modelling her new costume as an icon of bodily perfection before she, too, took the plunge.

"It's a good job I checked that out for depth and underwater obstacles yesterday!" said Ash. "Let that be a warning to you all! You could have come up wearing an old bicycle or whatever!" Ash could be a boring old stick at times, but his training meant that safety and managing risk was always present in his mind.

They swam for a few minutes then soaped up and washed off. "Give yourselves a good scrub!" said Lisette "You have to be clean for Jesus," knowing that in a couple of hours they would be off for the Sunday morning ritual. In the meantime, all the dogs were duck- diving and spending a few seconds below the surface. It had become almost an obsession.

Lisette spoke, "Ash, darling. What have you been teaching these dogs whilst I was away? They seem to spend more time under the water than on top."

"No idea my love. I first noticed it yesterday. I said to them at the time that they must have met up with a mermaid, but they certainly seem to like doing it."

With the morning swim done, they walked back to the cottage where breakfast consisted of undyed smoked haddock and poached eggs with tea, toast and marmalade." The dogs had a ladle of the stew each with a handful of biscuit. Ash and Lisette listened to the news on the radio, then they got ready.

Sunday best was never the order of the day but Lisette wore a print dress and cardigan and Ash a blazer and tie, and off they went on the two-mile bike ride for the church service at 10 am. Odi ran along at the side because the Reverend Patrick Collins welcomed well-behaved dogs into the service although there was a limit on numbers with one per household lest the dogs outnumber the rest of the congregation. The other dogs knew the routine and went back to their guard post under the oak.

The Church of St Michael and all the Angels was on the estate but on the far eastern side close to the gate house where one of the underkeepers resided with his family. From there it was only a hundred yards to the edge of the village of Spelthorpe. The church dated back to the fourteenth century and had been initiated as a thank you to the Almighty for sparing the estate and village from the great plague that had devastated the rest of the country. An enlightened lord of the manor had adopted a policy of strict isolation and self-sufficiency and this had worked. With the plague over and a surviving labour force the estate had been in poll position to take advantage. Norfolk had been a rich county.

Exports of predominantly wool, as well as other agricultural produce to mainland Europe provided rich pickings that funded the construction. The churchyard was curiously maintained in a state of tidy untidiness with areas set aside for trees and wildflowers and old gravestone slabs to provide shelter for small creatures. There was a massive old yew tree that was probably two thousand years old as the inside was completely hollow with sufficient space for up to ten people. The graves were simple stones scattered in rough lines but not overly manicured. The older graves stood out with the typical skulls and cherubs in the design, and some dated back for three hundred years where the inscriptions were readable on the sheltered northeastern side of the church and around the ancient yew. Oddly in the far corner was a small patch set aside with simple stones with engraved names like Prince, Percival, Raven and Matilda – the names of treasured dogs of the estate – gone but never forgotten. Halfway between the ancient tiled lychgate and main door was the war memorial modelled on the standard Imperial War Graves Cross of Sacrifice bearing the names of the twenty-nine men and two women(nurses) from Spelthorpe who had served in the Great War and did not come home. The church was typical of the era – well constructed and cool inside with a crenelated bell tower that flew the cross of St George. There was sufficient capacity inside for up to 200 people with wooden pews and on each side of the two central aisles several box pews were earmarked for families or children to sit together. A number of windows were in stained glass and had been added over the centuries. There was a newly constructed church hall used for social events, but this was just outside of the estate off the road to the village about 100 yards further on and named the Memorial Church Hall. This had been sponsored by the earl in the aftermath of the war.

The modest vicarage was adjacent to the church hall, but it had a sizeable garden.

The Reverend Patrick – or Paddy as he liked to be known, had been the vicar at Spelthorpe since 1919. He was an unorthodox character but universally loved by his parishioners and the very opposite of his cold and pompous predecessor who had been persuaded to move on. Matters had not been helped by the former vicar's memorable words to the Spelthorpe Company as they left for France in 1914, "May God go with you. I will go as far as the railway station!"

Paddy's popularity had been helped by his appearance with his flowing white hair and beard. He looked like God and many of the young children thought he was God with his kindly ways, coupled with an ability to strike terror in those who misbehaved in a malicious way. All it took was a firm large hand gripping a shoulder and behaviour changed in an instant.

Paddy had been ordained into the Church of Ireland and worked with the urban poor in Cork but when an appeal for chaplains for the troops went out, he answered the call and took off for France early in 1916. Unlike many of his colleagues he had a reputation for going up to the front-line trenches to spend time with the soldiers as the shells and bullets flew through the air and on occasions he would go out into no man's land to bring back the wounded. This had gained him a Military Cross. As well as his Bible he would volunteer to carry supplies up to the front line particularly if jars of rum were going forward. These were marked up SRD – Special Rations Department or as the troops often complained "Seldom Reaches Delivery" but Paddy would explain that he needed something to take communion with the soldiers. He conducted many funerals and on the relatively few occasions when soldiers were executed for desertion, he would spend the night with them in the condemned cell providing what comfort there was to be had, along with some rum. Some would want to sing a hymn remembered from their Sunday school days. To them it was like a prayer and the Reverend Paddy would sing along with them until the end. Somehow Paddy ended up alongside the

Norfolk Regiment and came to the attention of the eleventh earl who as the former colonel of the regiment, would come out and visit his military family. The earl asked him if he would come to Spelthorpe at the end of the war. He agreed so strings were pulled and some months later he arrived. Paddy was never one for ecclesiastical dogma. He didn't go in for repetitive rituals other than when required for the 'hatched, matched or dispatched' but that was it. He didn't do politics indicating that meddling and turbulent priests so often get their just desserts. His message was a simple one of human kindness and he preached that not just from the pulpit but by his example throughout the estate and village. He knew his Bible inside out and had a meaningful text for every occasion. He had time for all, even if the message was not what they wanted to hear. He formed a bond with one of the war widows on the estate. She played the organ in church and helped him in any possible way. It was only a matter of time before he and Ruth married. Paddy only wore his official robes when he had to. For much of the time he was in bare feet or sandals in a simple gown, more like St Francis than a Church of England priest. He would work in the churchyard, never taking a day off but being out and about, he would sometimes be seen shrimping on the waters in the sunset, on a boat with the fishermen or foraging for wild fruits, mushrooms and nuts. It was a way of connecting with God through nature and with others he encountered on his rounds. His other passion was for animals whom he saw as companions created by God and he refused the conventional doctrine that animals did not have souls. His own dog was a gentle black Irish wolfhound called Gelert, adored by the children of the village because of his size. Paddy's leadership was infectious and there was never any shortage of volunteers to help on the way. Some in the church hierarchy looked down on his maverick ways, but Paddy's universal popularity as the man who glued the community together with the full support of the earl ensured his immunity from scornful Church of England elders.

A few minutes before 10am the family parked their bicycles behind the church and entered. Earl Simon, Helen and the children sat in the boxed pew at the front. Julian Johnson and family were opposite and Ash, Lisette and the twins sat in the box behind the earl. Michael winked at Victoria as she turned to look back. They hadn't seen each other for a month. She smiled. There was clearly something stirring beyond a simple school friendship. Nods and handshakes were exchanged across the church.

Helen and Lisette had become close friends. Helen had met Simon in Kenya when he was a lieutenant in the Norfolks. Her father had made a fortune in India and now had extensive tea and coffee plantations in the Highlands just north of Nairobi. This was a time when some wealthy aristocrats and entrepreneurs with time on their hands had started to drink to excess and engage in salacious behaviour which in a few years' time would develop into what was known as the infamous Happy Valley Set. The young Helen had been approached on several occasions and was fearful, so when the dashing young lieutenant turned up she sought refuge with him and her father was relieved to see her escape the excesses of some of the neighbours. A few months later they were engaged and when Simon returned to Norfolk in 1912, she came home with him but had insisted that two loyal family servants whom she had known since childhood go along with her. Amrik and his wife Jasmir were Sikhs and following the wedding they were installed as a footman and assistant housekeeper within the Spelthorpe household. Over the years their loyalty, dedication, ability and diplomacy had earned them respect across the estate so when the long-serving butler retired at the age of sixty-five it was Amrik who was appointed to the position. In the meantime, Jasmir had taken on the management of the estate shop in the village that supplied the area's residents, dealing in the produce of the estate as well as items brought in to provide a more comprehensive supply. Reverend Paddy had made it absolutely clear that they were more than welcome to attend all events arranged through the church even if that meant abstention from a few items, but they came to the weekly service and other events where they were welcomed with enthusiasm. The weekly service started on time. There were always a few rousing hymns, and Reverend Paddy normally chose what the congregation could sing with gusto and without having to look at the words. '*He who would valiant be*' and '*All things bright and beautiful*' were always popular and in a couple of weeks '*We plough the fields and scatter*' would be at the top of the agenda as the harvest festival marked the conclusion of a busy time that had involved both regular workers and extras drafted in from the village. The vicar kept sermons and prayers short and to the point. It was not his job to bore people into sleep, and as far as he was concerned prayers consisted of ideas and things people might want to pray for in private because that was what Jesus had instructed. In his sermons he would explain many of the contradictions in the good book to make it meaningful. He was of the view that even God had a boredom threshold and prayers in the form of religious nagging with a shopping list of moans were hardly going to get results. Paddy's emphasis was always on thanks and comradeship, and he encouraged all in the congregation, regardless of their station in life, to shake hands especially with new arrivals and visitors. A communion service was held every two weeks. This was the unpretentious style he had adopted in the trenches, and it went down well here.

Ash, Lisette and the twins had sat in the box pew with the door open, but curiously instead of laying down as was usual and sleeping, Odi had spent the entire hour sitting up at the entrance to the box with her eyes firmly fixed on the stained-glass window with the image of the mermaid that was on the other wall. This had been gifted by the local guild of fishermen many decades back. It was very unusual behaviour and Lisette intuitively connected it with the duck diving display and Ash's comment when they were at the lake.

At the end of the service, they did not hang around so after observing customary politesse, they departed and within ten minutes had ridden back to the cottage. There were plans for the afternoon.

7

A miracle at sea

The return from church found the five dogs waiting under the oak. Earlier they had sneaked off as two and then three to meet Minerva at the pool for more underwater training. More was lined up for the following week.

Ash wanted to make this a special day. Being the last full day before returning to school and with Michael and Lucy away for a month he felt the need to bond with them again. Lunch was a quick sandwich then Ash loaded the back of the truck with the fishing rods and some ginger beer and selected the two senior dogs to go with them. Trooper and Rafe were both very steady and less excitable than the others, so they made ideal boat companions. Lisette had elected to stay behind to prepare a special evening meal and to take the time to write to her parents in Normandy to thank them for the splendid time they had given the twins.

The fishing party took off with the twins and dogs riding in the back of the truck down to the boathouse. It looked like a perfect day with no wind and Ash hoped that the weather would remain for the next few days as the second hay cut had taken place a week ago. It was dry and needed collecting. Sunday was always treated as a day of rest and relaxation on the estate unless there was a matter of real urgency. The hay harvest would be an all-hands job to get it undercover as winter feed for the livestock.

There was a compact fifteen-foot dory with oars and a sail in the boat house. Ash attached a British Seagull outboard motor because there was no wind. Four kapok filled life jackets were packed under the seats and without much of a do they set off. They powered out for the half mile along the inlet between the buoys that marked the channel and out into the open sea for another half mile into the deeper water where they drifted in a light current that took them west along the coastline. After a mile of drifting, they could make out the gap in the dunes and the roof of the cottage. Ash had two rods with traces made up with six hooks tied with chicken feathers with old spark plugs as weights that took the lines down, so they bobbed up and down between ten and twenty feet on each side below the boat. This had always worked before. Michael and Lucy had a rod each dropping the line down and jigging it up and down to make a movement in the water, so the hooks and feathers appeared like small bait fish. Trooper lay on a mat at the bow taking in the sunshine, but Rafe remained ever watchful of what was going on. They tried and tried but with no success. Ash moved on where he saw seagulls hovering above the water and terns diving, but still nothing happened. After an hour Rafe got up and looked over the side. He appeared fixed at something in the water. It was Minerva but she was totally invisible to Ash and the twins. Trooper came across.

"You are in the wrong place," said Minerva "If you go out another two hundred yards to the right there's a massive shoal of what you are looking for."

"How will I tell them?" asked Trooper.

"I'll get them out there," said Rafe. "I'll show them like I do on the shoot when we are picking up." With that he pointed his body in a straight line over to the right and barked gently.

"What's that dog up to?" asked Ash. "Get down you daft bugger!"

"No! No!" said Lucy. "I think he's trying to tell us something. I've seen this with him before when we are on the shoot. He always knows where to go and he guides me like that. Rafe's got a sixth sense and he's nearly always right. When he sits down, we will be at the right spot."

"Well, I suppose if you don't try you don't succeed so I'll give it a go."

Ash powered the boat out to where Rafe was pointing and when the dog sat down, he cut the motor, and they drifted. The twins dropped their lines and almost instantaneously the rods shook violently. The twins wound away. It was a struggle and Ash had to give Lucy a hand. Up came six large glistening green, silver and black striped mackerel on each line. Some fish fell into the bottom of the boat and others had to be detached by hand and stunned by Ash's priest – an old police truncheon given to him by a former village constable. That done, it was a repeat performance: lines down, fish on, reeling in and again and again and again. There were about eighty mackerel in the bottom of the boat.

"That's it," said Ash. "We stop now! You must never take more than you need or can use".

At that point two seals appeared off the port (left) side and Ash tossed each one a fish. "No more," he said. "You have had one each and that will be your ration."

The rods were placed on board and the traces with the hooks were bagged to prevent any accidents. Barbed hooks were difficult to extract and sometimes they had to be pushed through until the barbed end could be cut off with pliers.

"I have to confess that dog is amazing," said Ash. "He pulled off that miracle and he didn't even go to church this morning. I won't doubt him again. If he pulls a stunt like that twice more, we will be calling him St Rafe. There's something very odd with these dogs and I can't work it out with all this duck-diving and Odi this morning fixed on that stained- glass mermaid. Anyway, it's time to get back. We are going to take a steady course back and you two are going to do it. Lucy, you can go first, and Michael can help me gut these fish. There's no point in taking them home when we can do it here and feed the gulls, the seals and fish at the same time. It's a lot cleaner too."

It took an hour to get back. Ash took out a couple of boards that fitted over each side and two razor-sharp knives each with a cork float on string. The gulls mobbed the boat to start but the dogs made sure they didn't get too close and once a steady stream of fish guts trailed the boat, that was where the gulls concentrated their efforts.

Back at the boat house they tidied up and put the fish in a barrel. The dogs and Michael got in the back and Lucy sat next to her father.

"We can't go back straight away because we have some deliveries to make," said Ash. It was the custom to share out any bounty from nature so first, they stopped off at the gatehouse and left half a dozen with the under keeper who had presented them with the venison. They spotted the Reverend Paddy in the churchyard with Gelert who came bounding up when he saw the truck. They all jumped down because Gelert was the type of dog they all wanted to hug. The vicar walked over wearing his brown woollen gown and sandals.

"Here Paddy. We've got these for you. Two each for you and Ruth and a couple for your mighty beast." Ash handed over the mackerel wrapped in some hessian sacking.

"Ah! 'Tis manna from heaven." Paddy responded. "You've done well. Did you cast your net on the other side?" He alluded to the biblical tale.

"Not quite Paddy. It was Rafe who pointed the way and barked to tell us where to go and drop our lines. He was spot on."

"The Lord moves in mysterious ways, and his four-legged angels do his bidding. I thank you for your kindness, Ash, but I thank the creator for all the good gifts around us."

They chatted for a few minutes while Gelert made the most of an encounter with the twins and the dogs. Then it was all onboard, and onwards to Spelthorpe Hall. Amrik the butler came to the door as he had seen them approach.

"Good afternoon, sir. I'm afraid the master and mistress are out visiting," he explained.

"Don't worry about that Amrik. I'll catch up with them tomorrow. We have something here for cook and you will not get fresher than this! I can give you twenty if that is enough."

Amrik retreated into the house and came back a couple of minutes later with a bucket. "Cook is delighted. Twenty will be just right."

So, the fish were handed over, and the process was repeated with half a dozen to JJ, the keeper and Ash's parents. The whole process reminded Michael of Horatio Nelson who was born only a few miles away at Burnham Thorpe. It was a bit like the distribution of prize money to the officers and crew that followed a sea battle with the capture of an enemy ship.

They got back to the cottage, and they all felt a bit dirty from the fish scales and the splatters from the gutting process. There were about thirty fish left. Lisette took two as a treat for the cats Duma, Swahili for cheetah and Chui, Swahili for leopard. The cats had been a gift from Countess Helen whose own Siamese cat SimbaJike (lioness) had produced kittens two years back.

Helen had given them all Swahili names because it reminded her about the happy side of her time in Kenya. Ash decided that the best thing for the remaining mackerel would be to smoke them, so he quickly mixed cold water with salt and brown sugar and placed the gutted and headless fish into the mix. He would leave them for twelve hours to absorb the brine mix then put them in his home-made brick and corrugated iron smoking oven first thing in the morning.

"Dinner will be ready in an hour and a half," said Lisette. With that Ash grabbed a big towel and the soap bar and he, the twins and all the dogs ran off down to the lake for a good scrub. Lisette dashed out producing the swimming costumes "You have to be decent on a Sunday," she added.

Within the hour all were back and looking a lot cleaner. After a change of clothes, the family sat down to dinner. Ash put an Al Bowlly record on the gramophone. Lisette had been busy. After a starter of some potted shrimps on toast with an onion relish, she produced a superb roasted leg of lamb, with roast potatoes, runner beans, courgettes, carrots and peas all gathered from the garden along with freshly made mint sauce and a tasty gravy. For dessert there was a blackberry and apple crumble with custard. To wash it down there was a fine Bordeaux claret. It was one of two that the twins had brought back from Normandy and the crowning glory was a bottle of the finest Normandy Calvados which would be strictly rationed and kept for special occasions. Scraps and some vegetables had been stewed for the dogs along with some wood pigeon breasts shot the previous week which they would get once it had cooled. It was a glowing example of the best the land of the estate could offer in terms of fresh and natural ingredients without recourse to the shops.

The twins were worn out by the excitement and the variety of the day. It was good to come home, and tomorrow, they would be meeting up with their school friends. The school was ten miles away, but the school had its own bus, and this would collect them together with the Johnson and earl's children from the Hall at 4pm. Thereafter for the rest of term the bus would deliver them back at 2 pm on Saturdays and collect at 7.45 am on Monday mornings other than on the two extended exeat weekends and the one-week half term at the end of October. By 8pm it was dark, and bedtime followed shortly after that.

8

'All is safely gathered in'

Monday 5th September 1932

Ash was up at the crack of dawn. He took the mackerel and dried them then lit the charcoal under the tray that was loaded with oak shavings. Then he placed the fish in the racks in the smoker. The cold smoke process would take about eight hours. Lisette and the twins came downstairs. There was no time for a swim as pressing farm work lay ahead. Hay cuts normally took place in May and again in August. The hay provided vital winter feed for livestock when the grass was growing slowly or not at all. Weather was critical in the process because damp hay would rot, or it could spontaneously combust. The hay had been cut by cutters towed by the estate's two tractors and the horse teams. That was a week ago and the dry weather had held. The hay had been turned three days ago and now after the last three warm days there was an urgency to gather it, stack it loose or bale it using the latest mechanical Ann Arbor balers that had been imported from America. This would create rectangular bales that were easier to transport and manage. Some would be stacked in small circular stacks up to twelve feet high with tarpaulins over the top to keep the rain out. Some would go to the hay barn where it would be compressed by a static machine into larger square bales. There were 200 acres set aside for hay.

August had been a busy month with the harvesting of cereals: wheat, barley, oats and spelt – the latter being grown mainly in medieval times giving the estate its name. Harvesting was hard work, and all the hours of daylight were used because it involved cutting, the making of sheaves that were left out in the fields in stooks and then thrashing using a steam-powered thrashing machine to get the grain. Finally, the straw had to be gathered to be baled or stacked for use as bedding for periods when livestock were kept inside. Everyone took part including the children from the estate and this was the reason why the summer school holiday lasted for well over a month. The younger children learnt, and the older ones gained a bit of extra pocket money.

Ash had a mug of tea, then grabbed a chunk of bread, ham and an apple and took off in the truck. Michael and Lucy had instructions to ride up to the hay fields on their bicycles straight after breakfast, but they would be coming back at 2 pm to get ready for the return to school. Lisette emerged from the house after breakfast. The dogs, who had been sleeping under the tree again, bounced up expecting a bit of breakfast along with Chui and Duma who had their tails raised and were rubbing against Lisette's legs. She gave the cats a half filet of raw mackerel each whilst the dogs sat in line in envy and frustration that the cats always got their treats first. Then the dogs got a portion of biscuit and the remains of the venison stew. She spoke to the dogs as she always did, not feeling that some might think she was a disciple of Doctor Doolittle. "I'm going to be busy this morning catching up on housework and getting things ready for the twins going back to school, so you'll all have to go off and amuse yourselves.

Three stay and three go off so take it in turns." She put up three fingers to emphasise the point.

Housework was not easy but at least the house was blessed with electrical power and a telephone. To make things easier, Lisette did have a German Miele electric rotor washer that consisted of a wooden barrel, with a motor for the rotor with a draining board and mangle fitted. Hot water still had to be boiled on the Aga but the water either came from the hand pump by the large kitchen sink or directly from the outside well. Living at the cottage could be more difficult than in a town but the advantages were the envy of many. Ash had indicated that he was going to build a water tower that would at least give them running cold water. Earl Simon was conscious of the fact that the Hall was so well appointed in comparison. He had approved the project, but farm priorities had to come first.

Ash was up at the hayfield at 7 am. Work had already started. There were two tractors with the latest balers and four large hay carts each drawn by two Suffolk Punch horses. Fortunately, the hay meadows were within easy reach of the hay barns and those used for housing of livestock in winter. The Suffolk Punch horses were magnificent. They were powerful but kind-natured and totally biddable. There were ten on the farm, and two were kept by the sawmills for day-to-day work in the forest. Two mares in foal remained at the stable and the forest horses had come up for the day. Before the Great War there had been twenty of these horses on the estate, but despite protestations six were commandeered for war work and more would have gone had it not been for the fact that the efficient working of the farm was recognised. Those horses had been used to drag the heavy guns about the battlefield. It remained an overlooked fact of the Great War that although eleven million men on all sides had been killed, eight million horses were also sacrificed. The six from

Spelthorpe did not return. Mechanisation was in full swing, and those lost horses were not replaced. At present time both horses and tractors were fully engaged, although most could see the writing on the wall.

Earl Simon and JJ had turned out too, and they were stacking bales on one of the carts as it went along the line behind the baler. Two foremen were directing: one in the fields and another down at the barns. They were experienced hands and things were going well. Wives and children were out too, raking up the hay into piles and two pitchfork men were tossing up to a stacker on the back of each cart. Michael and Lucy had joined the rakers. JJ's daughters, in their mid-teens, were each leading a horse team and the earl's three children were helping at the barns. The weather was perfect, with mare's-tail clouds in the sky reminding some of the proverb 'Mares' tails and mackerel scales make lofty ships to carry low sails'. They indicated a storm was on its way. Insects disturbed by the activity flew skyward to be snapped up by swallows fattening up for the long flight south. It was a total team effort and even Reverend Paddy had come along with Ruth and Gelert who entertained the youngest children whilst Paddy was raking up and singing out loud from the hymn 'Bringing in the sheaves. We shall come rejoicing, bringing in the sheaves,' – and they did!

At noon Countess Helen appeared driving one of the estate's Ford trucks. She was loaded with sandwiches and bottles of beer and cider for the workers and ginger beer for the children. They all sat down for half an hour as brothers and sisters of the land they served – the land that sustained them in return. The two Johnson girls had their sandwiches but made sure that the horses had a drink and some oats in nose bags.

Back at the cottage the dogs had taken turns to go to the pool to meet up with Minerva. They related the previous day's success with the fishing and how they had been practising their underwater skills at every opportunity. Minerva said that the time had come for their final test. She dropped the oyster shell in the deepest part of the pool. It was twelve feet deep. The Labradors all managed it with relative ease, but Odi found it harder. On the third attempt she did it and they all managed to stay under the water for thirty seconds. "You have done brilliantly," said Minerva. "And because of that you are now all officially merdogs. I have worked my powers on you. You can now see clearly under the water and have better webbing between your toes. Over time you will stay down for longer and go deeper still but you must keep up the practice. When I see you again, I will take two of you on a journey and if that works out, we can do lots more."

The twins resumed work for an hour and then left on their bicycles to go back to the cottage. When they arrived Lisette was hanging out the washing which was drying rapidly in the warm breeze. Lisette sent them both up for a quick dip in the lake to clean off and the dogs went with them. Half an hour later they were back. Their bags were packed and the twins ensured that they had the project work that they had undertaken in the holiday. Michael had studied Norman castles and Lucy had written about coastal landforms. Their time in France had been useful and to really impress their teachers, both projects had been written in French. They were lavishly illustrated with photos they had taken.

At 3.30 pm they all left in the Morris and went up to the Hall. They wore their school uniforms with the distinctive mid-blue blazer. On arrival, they met up with the others who had also made the rapid transformation from farm workers to scholars at a prestigious school. The bus duly arrived, and they took off without any long goodbyes. The school had made them independent, and they had a lot of catching up to do with their school chums. Michael sat next to Victoria on the coach at the back, away from the others. They discreetly held hands – young love!

With the children gone the mums sighed with relief. Lisette took a bag from the boot. It contained her sports clothing and a tennis racket. The three mums had pre-planned a round-robin of singles tennis, with the non-player acting as umpire. They played for an hour then showered off and sat on the terrace overlooking the lake that lay to the northeast of the Hall. This lake was fed by the stream that drained the eastern side of the estate from south to north. The overflow from here continued down to the second lake near the cottage. Amrik arrived with a tray and a jug of Pimm's. It was serene and relaxing as they took in the view and continued with their girl talk. The lake was blessed with weeping willows and alders and the parkland between the lake and the Hall had two very impressive Lebanon cedars and several oaks. The stables and paddocks were quite close to the lake. The two pregnant mares who had missed the working party were grazing along with two donkeys, two Welsh mountain ponies and four Welsh cobs used for riding about the estate. The sky was starting to cloud over from the west although it remained warm. The mare's tails had gone and were being replaced by huge anvil-shaped cumulonimbus thunderclouds that rose up thousands of feet into the sky. The signals were there. It had been a splendid end to the day and the time had come to depart.

Lisette got back to the cottage. She fed the dogs and got Odi to do the chicken round-up and gathered some vegetables from the garden. The washing was dry. At 7.30pm Ash came back. He was sticky and dusty. "Well," he said. "We got it all done and in the nick of time by the look of it."

"You look like you could do with a good wash." She grabbed soap and a towel, and they walked down to the lake with the dogs in tow. Ash splashed and soaped up then entered the water and dipped below the surface. The total immersion relaxed and soothed him, and he remained motionless, totally relaxed. It slowed his heartbeat and his need for air. After a full minute he surfaced. Lisette was sitting on the bank with the dogs alongside. It was clear they had been swimming and had no further appetite to do so as it was late, and the darkness was darker still with the heavy cloud cover. They talked about their respective days and the work ahead. There was always something but that was the life they had made for themselves. At least it had its compensations. They were in constant touch with nature. They were never bored, and they had the best friends of all, real friends they could rely on and a family which included the canine and feline members too. Michael and Lucy were confident, self-reliant and strong, and that was what they wanted for them. There was stillness and silence apart from owls tweeting in the pines.

Suddenly the whole sky lit up. They counted slowly and waited for the bang. It came half a minute later – six miles away. The next flash was closer – four miles, then two and finally, it was almost instantaneous, but it failed to provoke any fear. After what they had both been through, they had both accepted a fatalistic view of destiny. It brought back memories of that night fourteen years back in May 1918 when they had been lovers. They were sitting in uniform on the banks of the Canche River at Étaples when the Hun had bombed the Canadian hospital. There were deaths: nurses, soldiers and patients. They had survived that. They remembered the carnage when they got to the scene and the efforts they and others had made to save and preserve life. They remembered the funerals, the sadness and the inevitable hatred that came from an attack on what was well-known as a hospital, but it was a training ground too, and for men who were destined to stem the German offensives that had driven the front line back almost as far as Amiens. Those same men would attack in August with renewed vigour, supported by the industrial might of the Allies to drive the Germans back to win the war in just a hundred days.

Then came the rain, slowly at first but then in torrents. They walked back slowly resigned to the fact that, soaked as they were, they could not get any wetter. The dogs walked into the barn and settled on the straw along with the cats. Ash and Lisette went inside and had a supper of smoked mackerel, salad and new potatoes. Two small glasses of the precious Calvados were consumed, and then they too, retired to bed.

9

England expects

On the following day Ash and Lisette were up at daybreak. As the tide was still far out, they all went back to the lake where the heavy night rain had brought the water level up by about four inches with the direct rainfall coupled with the input from the stream that fed it, and this was in full flood. Time was pressing so after fifteen minutes in the water they returned. They took a breakfast of boiled eggs and toast and after feeding the dogs and cats they both left. Ash took the truck as he was going up to the south side of the estate to see the gamekeeper known to all as Boynton or Mr. Boynton, but those who worked under his direction always called him Guvnor and he was happy with that. He had a first name, Aurelius, which he didn't like, and kept it secret.

Lisette went on her bicycle to the Hall. On this occasion she left Odi with the others.

The dogs knew the routine. They sat in the barn by the big twin doors as there were puddles everywhere and watched as the chickens scratched in the mud looking for worms.

The newly qualified merdogs waited for an hour and then decided which two would go off with Minerva on the journey she had promised. There was no debate. Trooper, as senior dog, had decided that he was going first, and number two Rafe was going too, so they trotted off through the gap and along the beach. When they got to the pool Minerva was waiting for them.

"Good morning merdogs. Have you been practising?" she asked.

"Indeed, we have," said Trooper. "And so much so, that Master and Mistress have noticed things and are starting to get suspicious."

"I wouldn't worry about that," she responded, "They can't see me and never will, so they will just put it down to you lot being a clever bunch and will get used to it. Today is going to be your first journey. We are going to go a long way, but it won't be far. Now there's a riddle for you, but all will become clear once we arrive at our destination. If you are ready, all I want you to do is to dive to the bottom of the pool with me and then my powers will kick in. It will take just a few seconds."

Both dogs wagged their tails with enthusiasm, and as Minerva dived to the bottom of the pool, they followed her down. Everything went hazy for a couple of seconds, and then it was perfectly clear, and they surfaced. They looked around them. They were still in the same pool, so they hadn't gone anywhere, but when they looked again the things around them were different. All the pines had disappeared, but the dunes were still there. They looked further along where they could normally see the road and railway line in the distance at the point where it got close to the coast, but that was not there. They looked out to sea and saw three ships heading west about two miles out, but these ships just had lots of sails and no funnels or smoke. Walking towards them was a young boy. He appeared to be about eight or nine years old, but he was quite skinny and wiry and had a look of determination and purpose about him. His hair was a light brown and tied back in a short ponytail. His feet were bare, and

67

he wore just a pair of canvas trousers that went just below the knee, a grey shirt and a navy-blue canvas cotton jacket. He kept looking out to sea and was concentrating on the ships.

He walked up to them and said without the slightest surprise "Hello. Mermaid and dogs!" To him mermaids were perfectly normal as he had seen many before on the front of ships. The sailors believed that whilst having a woman on a ship could bring bad luck, a bare- breasted mermaid on the prow would have a calming effect on rough seas and bring good luck.

"And where have you come from young man?" asked Minerva.

"Oh. I live in the village about three miles over there. It's called Burnham Thorpe. My father is the rector of the church. I like to get out if I can because I have ten brothers and sisters, and they can annoy me at times. I come here to look for any ships that go past. Those three out there are merchantmen bound for King's Lynn but sometimes I see a frigate, a fighting ship. That's what I like," the boy responded.

"So, you like the sea then? I suppose you want to join the navy?" asked Minerva.

"Of course, and I will. My Uncle Maurice has promised me that. He is my mother's brother, and he is a famous navy captain, Captain Suckling. In three years' time when I am twelve he said that he would get me on a ship as a midshipman. I will spend a few years learning everything about the sea and ships. Then after my examinations they will make me a lieutenant and sooner or later I will be a captain with a ship of my own, a frigate to start with, and I will be able to go out to hunt and destroy the French. I will get lots of Frog ships as prizes. My mother says that you must hate a Frenchman like the devil."

"You seem very determined about that," commented Minerva.

"I am, and I know I'm going to do it. When you are in the

navy, you must attack the Frogs every time you see them, and to win you need a good crew who are fast and accurate on the guns and with a good captain. The navy doesn't like cowards. My uncle told me that about 10 years ago they shot an admiral who made off and didn't attack the enemy. I won't be like that. Anyway, it was good to meet you all and I hope you will bring me luck. I have to go now because they will expect me back soon."

"You will be lucky!" said Minerva. "And by the way the dogs Trooper and Rafe would like to know your name".

"I am Horatio, Horatio Nelson." And with that he turned and walked back the way he had come giving them a wave as he disappeared into the dunes.

Minerva turned and beckoned the dogs to dive down with her into in the pool. Things were blurred for a couple of seconds and when they surfaced, they were back where they started. It was reassuring to see the pines and the marram grass on the dunes again. Minerva addressed them both. "Now you can answer my riddle. We didn't go far but we went a long way, A long way back in time, 175 years, in fact. What did you think about that?"

The dogs wagged their tales and asked if Minerva knew what happened to the boy.

She responded. "He did everything he said he would do. When he was only twenty, he became a captain, and he went on to be England's greatest-ever admiral. He fought the French and Spanish even though they outnumbered the ships he commanded, but he won battle after battle. At his greatest battle. the one that saved England from invasion, he was killed by a Frenchman's bullet. But the battle was won because of his plan and before he died, he thanked God that he had done his duty."

Trooper asked, "So you took us back in time. That was interesting but could you take us into the future?"

The main deck HMS *Victory* at Portsmouth

"I could but that is something I must never do. To take you forward might tempt you to change history, and that is simply impossible and frustrating. What has happened is set and so too is the future, but to take you forward would give you a special knowledge of how things would work out, and that could upset you and might make you behave in an odd way to others. With special knowledge of the future, some people might be tempted to cheat on things. None of that would be fair. We must live one day at a time and make the most of every day because every day is a gift. Going back is just a living history lesson to be enjoyed and experienced. Importantly, it will help you understand why things happened and in greater depth and it can help you make wise decisions as you live your lives. Others can read about things that have happened and act in a similar way, but because you are Merdogs you can see it happen for yourselves."

"That sounds very sensible," said Rafe. They both thanked Minerva for what she had shown them. Trooper indicated that they had to go back to the cottage. Minerva suggested that the next pair come and see her in a few days, but they should explain to the others what was involved. She said they should rest for a few days and go back to being ordinary dogs again until the next time, but underwater swimming practice would be good. With the changes to their eyes, they would see much more clearly.

Ash had gone up early to see Boynton who lived on his own with his two dogs in a cottage on the southern part of the estate on the edge of the woodland by the pheasant rearing pens and the deer park. Two underkeepers worked under him. One lived in the eastern gatehouse and the other in the southern gatehouse. Between them as well as gamekeeping they managed the herd of 500 deer in the parklands and acted as the security of the estate with Ash exercising that function in the northern coastal zone. For that reason, all houses had a telephone. The pheasant shooting season would be starting in less than a month and Ash needed to check that everything was in order and if Boynton needed any help. Boynton's team had released some 5,000 pheasants on the estate and a similar number of partridges which was a lot less than the huge numbers shot before the Great War. At the present time, they were preoccupied with keeping the birds on the estate by feeding them at key points where drum feeders were placed, and grain was scattered. Not to do this would mean that the birds would fly off to other estates to get fed and those who had done nothing to rear the birds would shoot them. The object was to encourage the birds to remain. Predators like foxes had to be controlled. A few were acceptable but balance had to be maintained. The same applied to rabbits and wood pigeons who would decimate seeded areas and growing cereal crops. The estate was small in pheasant shooting terms, but it allowed for up to twenty organised days throughout the season that lasted until the end of January. The earl would invite friends and associates to shoot on five of the days and the remaining days were sold to a shooting agent who would pay for days after indicating the number of birds to be shot. This helped to defray the costs of the shooting side of the estate business. In return, the earl would get invited to go either alone or with a guest to other shoots across the country.

The shoot was popular in the locality with most shoot days taking place on Saturdays. Boynton had to arrange for beaters to drive the pheasants forward and Ash took charge of the team of pickers who would work their dogs to retrieve dead and wounded birds. The beaters would earn five shillings expenses a day and the pickers six shillings plus a meal and a pint in the pub for the lunchtime break whilst the guns and guests enjoyed their three courses and drinks in the Hall. For the youngsters of the village, it was a bit of pocket money and a good day out. Any pheasants not taken by the shooters would be sold and there was always the odd one left over for the beaters or pickers.

Ash and Boynton went back a long way to when they were boys on the estate. Boynton had lived in the village and would come up regularly as a beater on shoots, but when he was ten, his father, who was a sergeant major in the Royal Engineers, was posted to Egypt and because of his senior position, was allowed to take his family with him. It was a welcome opportunity to get some all-year sunshine although the summer heat could be unbearable at times and the flies were everywhere. They had a particular liking for the army-issue apricot jam, which seemed to be the only jam that was ever available. The family lived in a closed community not far from Cairo, but the young Boynton managed to get out as much as possible to explore. With his tanned complexion he did not stand out too much, and he adopted the local dress. He made friends with some of the local boys and was soon speaking Arabic with an astounding level of fluency. After five years the family came home, and Boynton senior left the army. With his engineering experience, his dad filled a place on the estate maintenance team and Boynton gained a job as a trainee underkeeper. He worked his way up in the role and had joined the Spelthorpe company. When war came, he went off with them as a private but when the company was split after the Aubers Ridge fiasco the army found out that he was fluent in Arabic so he found himself posted to the intelligence branch in Cairo with the rank of sergeant. In 1917 Boynton found himself behind the lines attached to a unit commanded by the scruffiest major in the British army who was working with Arabs stirring up a revolt against their Turkish masters with whom the British were at war. Major Lawrence was small in stature but was a hero to the Arabs. They called him Al Aurens. He was totally irregular and had no time for rank or military pomposity and adopted Arab dress in preference to uniform. Boynton had found something that he could excel at and was a kindred spirit to Al Aurens. The small unit working with the Arabs spent the time blowing up Turkish railway lines and bridges and terrorising the Turks at every opportunity only to disappear back into the desert. They took few prisoners. Their methods were not in the military rule book, but the results were spectacular. In 1919 Boynton was demobbed but came home briefly and found time to bury a large bag of military hardware in the Spelthorpe Woods. Over the last two years at war, he had become addicted to living on the edge so within two months of his return he found himself in Ireland as one of the infamous Black and Tans where he applied the skills learnt in the desert enabling him to beat the Irish Flying Columns at their own game. The desert war had taught him to make himself invisible and how to use and exploit the ground to the maximum extent. With Irish peace negotiations in 1921, Boynton returned to Spelthorpe and managed to get his job back and after five years he was promoted to the estate's keeper when the incumbent retired. Boynton was a workaholic when it came to his gamekeeping. Stealth was second nature to him, and he had a way of surfacing where he was least expected. This reputation kept any poachers away. He didn't suffer fools gladly and his language was packed with Anglo Saxon expletives. Every alternate word was a swear word, although he had the remarkable ability to switch that off if ladies were present, but he did have a sense of humour. His two Labrador bitches, one black and the other fox red, he named Black and Tan. His rough and ready ways, coupled with a unique charm made him attractive to some. He never married but formed close relationships with some of the estate's war widows. Always discreet, he would visit in darkness. The ladies would indulge him with a meal, and in return he would fulfil their needs for nocturnal companionship.

Ash and Boynton took a drive around the southern end. Although the feeders were out, the pheasants and partridges were drawn to the cereal stubbles where rich pickings were to be had. A large number of wood pigeons were also feeding there. These had to be reduced in number, and this would be carried out by shooting over decoys on the stubbles and then throughout the autumn and winter by flight shooting as the birds looked for a roost in the couple of hours before darkness. Ash had no interest in shooting pheasants. Anyone could hit a low-flying bird that flew in a straight line but pigeon shooting required concealment and real skill because the birds were ever watchful and would swerve violently at the slightest movement. That provided a real challenge. The kale and turnip cover crops were doing well. These had a dual purpose. They provided shelter for the birds but at the end of the season the sheep would go in to enrich their diet during the gestation period. A herd of some 300 fallow and 200 red deer were maintained in the parkland and some of the fully wooded area. As numbers went above that, there would be a periodic cull that Boynton and his underkeepers would carry out. Most of the venison was sold to local game dealers and butchers. The estate managed a small slaughterhouse and butchery for local needs, but the bulk of the farm's livestock were taken by train to King's Lynn for the livestock market. Ash and Boynton got on well. Ash allowed Boynton to do things his way because he got results, and he supported him if there was a need for any extra equipment. There was only ever an occasional need to adjust priorities when balanced against other requirements of the estate, and Boynton fully understood that.

In the afternoon Ash went down to the edge of the wooded area close to the foresters' workshops. Several paddocks held some 200 Tamworth pigs. This was a new venture on the estate and a new line for John Sharpe, the coastal stockman, who was not exactly overworked by the Highland cattle and marsh sheep who managed themselves for the bulk of the time. The Tamworths were entertaining, hardy and self-contained pigs. They stood out with their red – brown colour. Although slower growing, their meat was rated the most flavoursome but they were very active and liked to root out woodlands. Over the last few days, the foresters and stockman had worked to fence out a thirty-acre area of woodland where the pigs could rummage and feast on the acorns. This was an ancient tradition called pannage and in many other parts of the country had been going on since medieval times when it was a privilege for local peasants to allow their pigs onto common land and royal forests. Ash walked along the fence line. It was sturdy, so over the afternoon they moved the pigs from the paddocks into the forest. It was not as difficult a task as he imagined. The pigs were curious and followed and once the herd could hear the squeals of delight from the first pigs into the woodland the rest followed on quickly. This venture would not only cut down on the feed bill but would also improve the soil structure in the wooded areas. Ash took tea with John and the forest men and congratulated them on a job well done, then he returned home to the cottage.

Having been left all day the dogs were pleased to see the return of their master. Mistress had prepared an evening meal, but first, relaxation was required. The tide had come in and gone out again over midday, so the lake seemed the best option. With nobody about, both opted to swim au naturel. They both preferred it that way, it seemed more relaxing and provided a harmonious link with all the trees and wildlife around them. They would swim out to the deeper water and allow themselves to slowly sink as there was far less buoyancy than the sea. Pulses would slow and a minute of submersion was easy, but this time they were no longer totally alone as the merdogs would dive down and show off by swimming around them like huge ginger otters. They stayed for an hour and talked as the sun set. After the excitement and activity with the twins return, diversions like this were restorative. The darkness was noticeably earlier than a week ago. They walked back to the cottage arm in arm in the twilight.

10

An evil visitation

For the rest of the week a sense of normality returned. There was plenty of work on the farm and woodlands. There were ten acres of potatoes to supply local needs and the estate shop. These would be harvested and stored along with carrots and other vegetables. Most of the workers in tied cottages had generous gardens and a system of mutually beneficial barter had developed over time. The shop would purchase any surpluses at the going rate. Chicken keeping was encouraged. In the orchards most of the apples had been picked, and the drops were gathered by the workers and families on Saturday afternoon for the annual cider-making tradition. This created a benefit supplied to households at a minimal charge. Several barrels were retained for free distribution at farm gatherings and social events over the year ahead.

The children all returned from school on the Saturday. The project work submitted by the twins had been exceptionally well received. They were now only a few weeks from their teens. Increased signs of transformation into adulthood were emerging in respect of their independence, self-reliance and determination. Periodically, there were challenges to the rules, but this was only expected. Calmness and encouragement to see think things through usually prevailed. At times Michael would disappear, and this was mirrored at the Hall when Victoria would do the same. Lisette kept a watchful eye but at a distance.

The dogs managed themselves in the usual way. The daily swims continued, and contact with Minerva was maintained. Hunter and Odi were lined up for the next trip and this should be easier, as in term time, Lisette tended to leave Odi with the others. Ash took Nimrod out shooting pigeons when he had a couple of hours free on one afternoon. This was an area where Nimrod came into his own and fulfilled the meaning of his name as 'mighty hunter'. After Ash had placed a dozen decoys, he would sit in the straw bale hide set into a hedgerow or on the edge of woodland. As soon as Ash stood up to shoot, Nimrod's head would emerge to see outside. When a wood pigeon was hit, Nimrod raced out like a guided rocket and was on the bird, often before it hit the ground. If a bird went down in the trees, again he was on it. He would vanish into the wood only to emerge seconds later with the bird in his mouth and run back to the hide to deposit the bird and to be ready for the next. He was a total natural. Training had been minimal. It was something he was bred for and what he wanted to do. The bag was forty-five, and the usual distribution took place on the journey back. Ash's rule was that anything taken could be used and it had to be used. Killing purely for shooting's sake was totally wrong in his book. Clay targets existed for that sort of thing, and it was a useful way of ensuring that those who wanted to shoot knew how to do it efficiently before heading into the countryside.

In mid-September on a Tuesday morning the telephone rang in the cottage at 7 am. Ash shouted up the stairs, "Lisette! Have got to dash. Something bloody awful has happened to the sheep. I'll explain later. I'll take Trooper and Rafe." He threw his clothes on and grabbed his binoculars before jumping in the truck.

It took Ash ten minutes to get up to the far southeastern corner of the estate. There were several small fields of less than ten acres surrounded by hedgerows with trees or the outer estate wall on one side. These were used in rotation for crops and grazing. He saw a couple of trucks and a car at the entrance gate, indicating that others were present.

Simon was there with JJ, along with Amos the shepherd who looked after the estate's flock of 1,000 sheep. Reverend Paddy and Boynton had also turned up. There was also a rotund figure in a navy blue uniform and police helmet. Ash had nothing but contempt for Constable Snodgrass. Spelthorpe was one of ten villages on the constable's patch and the only thing that could be said was that on some occasions, he attended. Snodgrass had been in post for the last five years and had achieved nothing other than increasing the size of his belly and feathering his nest in donations from locals who gifted items to him in the hope of a quiet life. He merely did the minimum in respect of what was expected but he lacked the killer instinct of a good copper who would seek to serve his people and lock up those who wrecked the quality of life of others. His predecessor John Skingle had been a first-rate thief-taker who left no stone unturned. Ash and he had got on well. They had worked together to produce excellent results, but that didn't last because his ability had come to notice of the police hierarchy. Within the last five years he had gone on to detective work and was now the detective inspector heading the CID at King's Lynn.

Amos had been the head shepherd on the estate for the last twenty-five years. He was kind and conscientious in the extreme. Nobody understood sheep more than he. Amos was visibly shaken, and tears were in his eyes.

Ash walked into the field. He uttered just one word.

"Bastards!" Sheep carcasses littered the ground. Throats had been torn out; some were partially disembowelled. Others ran around, bloodied in a continuing state of panic. About fifty were huddled together in a corner.

JJ asked, "What do you make of it, Amos?"

Amos answered. "I got here at first light to check them. There were a hundred in here ready for me to put the ram in. They were some of our best Suffolks – purebreds. I counted twenty-five dead. Most of those in the corner seem all right but we will have to check each one individually. Those wandering will be touch and go."

JJ responded. "I've got some of the stockmen coming up with hurdles. We need to get the good ones out of here as quickly as possible. Then we will have to sort out those who will not survive. I've called on the vet to come up, and if we can corral the wanderers, he will look at them one at a time. Boynton! Can you and the keepers deal with that side of it? I don't want Amos involved in that."

Boynton spoke. "We will deal with that, sir. I've noticed that we have six sets of intestines in a pile by the wall. Looks like they have partially butchered them after slitting their throats. That's to keep the weight down when they take them away."

Earl Simon asked. "Constable Snodgrass. What's your take on this? What are you going to do?"

Snodgrass responded as anticipated, "Well, my Lord. There's not a lot I can do. This is not the first in the district. It's happened a dozen places elsewhere."

Ash interrupted. "Not a lot you can do! You could have warned us about the others for a start! You could have looked for a geographical pattern. You could have knocked on some doors across the patch. Who is coordinating this? Have you told your seniors? This is not some isolated dog worrying issue. It's clearly an organised gang, even if the crudeness of their operation beggars belief. We've got twenty-five or more dead sheep here, and some of our best at that and just so these thieving bastards could take six away with them."

Snodgrass answered. "I suppose I could make some enquiries with local butchers to see if they have been offered any."

Ash was furious. "Better get on with it then and straight away!"

Snodgrass took the hint and got back on his bicycle. He was off.

Earl Simon spoke. "You got rid of him Ash. I get the impression you don't see eye to eye."

Ash responded. "You got that right. The man's as much use as a tub of lard. It seems that as he's no use they put him out to grass thinking that nothing ever happens in the countryside. We will have to try and sort this ourselves because in this instance the constabulary is not going to help, and the trail is getting cold. My instinct tells me that we will have to do it in a way that doesn't come back and bite us. These people are evil. I've got my two best trackers with me. I'm going over the wall near where they butchered them and hopefully there is a trail we can follow. If I come across anyone or anything I'll just be seen as a man taking his dogs for a walk. The quicker I do this the better."

Ash went back to get Trooper and Rafe. He made them walk to heel and skirted the edge of the field so as not to alarm the sheep then they all got over the wall at the point Boynton had indicated.

Reverend Paddy offered his help to Boynton, who was sorting the sheep. Boynton was fuming inside at what had taken place and the fact that he hadn't been able to stop it but on an estate of some twelve square miles that would have been an impossibility without any indication, and that had not been forthcoming. Boynton resorted to his colourful language and then realised that Paddy was a man of the cloth. "I'm sorry about my words, Reverend," he said, "but I just can't express myself in any other way."

"Oh, don't you be a worrying about that, my son. When I was in the trenches, I heard far worse than what you are coming out with. I remember a Belgian priest came up to me once. Said he couldn't understand why all the British and Irish soldiers kept complaining that Belgium was not real because it was fake. When I asked him what he meant by that he told me that they kept saying 'fake Belgium' and 'faking Belgium.' After I explained he was a bit shocked, but he saw the funny side of it. I just hope that the good Lord will strike down whoever did this. 'Vengeance is mine' said the Lord. All I can say is that it is for God to take revenge but that may be in the next world."

Boynton responded. "Well perhaps God needs someone in this world who might help them on their way to the next world. I seem to remember that your book says a lot about looking after the sheep. Perhaps God needs a servant who can help him."

"That may be so, Boynton," said Paddy. "Indeed, the Lord moves in mysterious ways and who are we to question that?"

Together they managed to pen the loose sheep. The vet arrived in half an hour and marked those that had to be destroyed and those who would make it with care. A dozen were taken to a neighbouring field where wounds were sprayed with an iodine solution and the vet stitched them there and then with help from Paddy and one of the stockmen. Boynton and the underkeeper dispatched those beyond hope. The carcasses from the field, along with those dispatched, were loaded into a truck – forty-two in total. They drove down to the slaughterhouse where any useable meat would be salvaged for dog food with the remainder incinerated in a pit.

On the other side of the wall, blood and wool showed where the stolen sheep had been dragged. Crushed vegetation indicated that they had used wheelbarrows. Ash put long tracking leads on the dogs and gave the command. "Track! Track!" They took off at a pace with Ash running behind. They crossed fields and after half a mile came across an old droving road. It was partially sunken with hedges and trees on each side. They followed the road for a hundred yards and came across a wider turning area where again blood, wool and tyre marks were present showing where the carcasses had been loaded into a lorry of some sort. Ash and the dogs walked along the track with crushed vegetation showing the route. He took the tracking leads off the dogs and walked at a fast trot. Ash looked at his watch. It was 8.30 am. After forty-five minutes there appeared to be a wide, flat expanse of common land. Ash stopped and then walked slowly forward using the hedgerow as cover. He noticed what looked like a parked green ex-army lorry with a canvas awning about a hundred yards away across the flat area. Next to it was a living van in a brown colour.

Ash took out his binoculars and scanned the area. There were two males. One appeared to be in his fifties, and the other in his mid-twenties. Both had a swarthy outdoor look about them. The younger man appeared to be gathering firewood whilst the older man was pulling dead sheep out of the back of the lorry. He was tying them up under the tree and stripping the fleeces off. There were clearly more than the six sheep Spelthorpe had lost. They had probably hit several flocks that night. The man hacked off the heads and flung them at two large dogs chained to the tree. They were large athletic dogs that looked like a cross between a lurcher and an Alsatian. Ash carried on walking along the drover's road, all the time scanning the area around the campsite. After half a mile the droving road connected to the highway and Ash recognised it as the lane that led to Fakenham five miles further on. He took a slow walk back hidden by the hedgerow and waited. On measuring the wheelbase, Ash could tell there were no signs of any other vehicles using the drovers' road. He waited and watched for another hour, then made his way back the way he had come.

Just before midday he was back on the estate and driving down to the Hall. On the way, he encountered Boynton, who was coming back from the slaughterhouse and butchery unit. Both stopped and got out. Ash explained all that he had seen and discovered. Boynton knew of the old drover's trail and the common area at the end. Ash said "I don't know how we go on from here. If we go to the police, they will take days to get organised and the birds will have flown. These types do not hang around for too long, but they are quite out of the way and feel safe at the moment. We have at the most twenty-four hours. The problem is that if we do not stop them, they will just carry on across the county and further. The police are parochial and will not be concerned. They are not up to dealing with travelling criminals. The other issue is if we strike, they must not know it came from us. I've seen it elsewhere when matters were reported. The police make a mess of it and then they come back with their mates to do untold damage, cutting fences, poisoning cattle and firing hay ricks."

Boynton responded. "I know where you are coming from. These men are evil bastards. I know the way they think. They are amoral. They care about no one but themselves. Fear is their weapon. There is only one way and that is to beat them at their own game making them so fearful they will never return and when they tell others they will stay away too. Deep down they are cowards. I will sort this. You do not need to know what I will do but I will make sure we never see them and their ilk again. Could I ask one thing?"

"What is that?" asked Ash.

"Don't tell his lordship what you have discovered. He might lose his bottle and go to the police and then we will be buggered. You know me. I'll sort it, but I have to do it my way, like I did in Jordan and in Ireland. If you don't know you can't tell. Can I have your word on that?"

Ash reflected for a few seconds, "Yes. Twenty-four hours. You have my word."

They shook hands. Boynton went to the back of the truck and produced two large legs of mutton. "That should feed your dogs for a week," he said.

Ash drove down to the Hall and felt a little guilty about not telling Simon he but remembered his officer's military training. He thought. It was all about the 'need to know' principle and at this time Simon didn't need to know because that would have given him a moral dilemma particularly as a magistrate. Leaving it to Boynton seemed the wisest course in the long term. Simon told him that he had rung around other farms and had discovered two others within a ten-mile radius that had been hit that night. One with sheep in a field by the main road had lost a dozen taken with another twenty dead or destroyed. Another farm had lost five, but those were the only sheep in the field. He intimated that he had spoken to the chief constable and was going to meet him the following week about Snodgrass and police cover in the rural parts of the county.

Ash just told him that he had followed a track to the main road and then lost it. Apparently, the birds had flown. Ash spent the rest of the day with Amos. He felt that he was vulnerable and needed to show him he had Ash's full support. In the late afternoon he returned to the cottage. They took the dogs to the lake and swam. He related the events of the day and his concerns but true to his word, he left out the bit about Boynton.

11

Nemesis

Boynton went back to his cottage. He walked Black and Tan and thought about his options. On his return, he fed the dogs with biscuit and large chunks of raw mutton meat, then he went into the barn and lifted a concealed trapdoor that was covered with straw. There was a damp-proofed and bricked hollow underneath that was packed with souvenirs from his days in the military. There was a Mauser sniper rifle, a standard issue Lee-Enfield rifle, a Browning automatic rifle and a selection of revolvers and pistols. There was plenty of ammunition as well as a selection of grenades: Mills bombs and German- designed stick grenades. There was also a bag with about forty caltrops – each with four spikes designed to stop horses or camels and anyone on foot. When dropped, one point was always upwards. He selected a Mauser broom handle pistol with a silencer. This had been the favourite weapon of Al Aurens in the desert. At the turn of the century Winston Churchill MP had also chosen one rather than a sword because of a shoulder injury received whilst he fought the dervishes on horseback in the Sudan. It was powerful, very accurate and had a big advantage over the six shot Webley revolver because of its ten-round magazine.

Furthermore, it could be reloaded from a strip in a couple of seconds. Boynton also took out two stick grenades taken from the Turks and the bag of caltrops.

He tested the Mauser. It worked perfectly.

Boynton placed everything in a dark canvas bag along with a set of black overalls, a black balaclava with just the eye holes, a pair of darkened desert boots that left no tread marks and a small battery torch. He walked to the southern end of the estate and just before sunset he changed his clothing. He hid his day clothes under a bush. There was nobody about. The full moon gave him all the light he needed. A medium breeze from the southwest made enough noise to disguise any sounds he might make.

He walked the three miles along the drover road and when he arrived at the point where the common land emerged, he sat and watched through a pair of binoculars. Both dogs were sleeping under the tree. They had probably spent the day feasting on sheep's heads. There was a light in the living van. He could hear voices from inside. He crept closer making sure he was downwind of the dogs. There were two voices from inside the van. They sounded like they had been drinking.

Boynton crept up to the dogs with the silenced Mauser in his hand. The noise of leaves rustling in the tree was handy. He got within six feet of the dogs and fired two silenced shots into the brain of each dog. They would kill no more sheep. Boynton picked up the empty cartridge cases. He crept up to the van and peered inside. Both men were lying on a couch with an empty bottle of rum on the table in front of them. He scattered the caltrops by the bottom of the steps to the van door. Boynton then walked over to the lorry that was parked close to the tree about twenty yards from the van. He looked in the back. It was packed with fleeces and about a dozen sheep carcasses. He took a stick grenade from his bag and unscrewed the bottom of the stick so the bead inside dropped down. He wedged the bomb between the fuel tank and the chassis then tied a length of string around the base of the bead and unravelled it for ten yards. He waited and watched and removed the silencer from the pistol. That would not be needed again. The living van was quiet. Boynton pulled the string, then ran and hit the ground after five seconds.

Two seconds later there was a huge explosion as the lorry was engulfed in a fireball from the blast incendiary created by the stick grenade and the petrol tank.

Boynton watched the door of the living van. A few seconds later, both men emerged shocked and in a panic as the lorry blazed away. They had no boots on. The first man, the younger one, stepped on a caltrop and screamed in agony. He fell and another pierced an arm. The older man did the same screaming and falling with another caltrop going through his right hand.

Neither man could stand, so they crawled as fast as they and their pain would allow them to get away from the heat of the lorry fire. They crawled in the direction of the drover's road both bleeding profusely with every movement an agonisingly painful one.

When they had gone about fifty yards, Boynton emerged from the darkness and stood in their path with the Mauser in his hand. He raised the Mauser and put a shot neatly through the right knee joint of each man. Both screamed again and curled up in agony.

It seemed longer, but after thirty seconds, the older man spoke. "Don't kill us. Please don't kill us. Who are you?"

Both men waited. Boynton spoke softly and deliberately with an Irish accent, "My name is Nemesis," and with that, he picked up both cartridge cases and walked back to the living van collecting and counting all the caltrops so there was no clue left as to his visit. He looked inside the van. There was a gallon of paraffin in a can, which he poured out. He went to the dogs and dragged each back and put them in the van, then he coolly took out the other stick grenade and tossed it into the van. He sprinted for five seconds, then dropped to the ground. After the explosion he calmly walked off with a satisfied grin with the living van blazing away as he disappeared into the darkness.

Before midnight Boynton was back. Black and Tan were pleased to see him. He replaced his equipment and washed his overalls and other clothing with washing soda. He walked the dogs for ten minutes took a large measure of Jameson's and went to bed. It had been a long day. Normality had returned. The following day he rang Ash. "All sorted," he said. "We won't see the likes of them again." – And they never did.

A week later, rumours got back of a massive fire of a lorry and living van near the Fakenham Road. Two men had been found crawling by the lane early in the morning having been kneecapped. In hospital they were both in a state of total terror. The police attended but both refused to say anything. They just wanted to get as far away as possible from Norfolk and gave the impression that somebody from Ireland was coming for them. Simon was suspicious. He spoke to Ash. "Do you know what this was all about? Did our Mr Boynton have anything to do with it?"

"Oh. I don't think so." said Ash as he smiled knowingly. "Boynton would never do such a dreadful thing. It must have been an act of God because Paddy kept on quoting the Bible 'Vengeance is Mine. I will repay, says the Lord.'"

After that nobody said a word.

Two days later, Earl Simon went out from the Hall on horseback for a ride about the estate with a parcel in his saddlebag. Boynton was out working filling the pheasant feeders. When he returned to his cottage there was a parcel on his step. He opened it to find a bottle of Jameson's Irish Whiskey and taped to it were three gold sovereigns.

12

Monkey business

Saturday 24th September 1932

Dawn found Lisette and Ash swimming in the sea with the dogs. The Indian summer was lasting well, although signs of autumn were apparent. The nights were colder, and the water temperature had just started to drop. The leaves on the horse chestnuts were starting to go yellow and brown. The leaves on the other trees would soon follow. Over the last few weeks Lisette and Countess Helen had been busy, out together with all the dogs, picking blackberries. The dogs were curious, and they too, started eating the low-lying fruit as they had done with the plums back in July. They picked the remaining Bramley apples. Between them, they had made forty jars of the finest blackberry and apple jam. Next, they were out picking the sloes from the blackthorn that abounded in the hedgerows. These had to be pierced and steeped in gin with sugar to make sloe gin, a favourite tipple for those on the shooting days. By mid-November, it would normally be ready although keeping it longer made it better still. It was tedious at times but after storage in glass demijohns and decanting, there was sufficient for fifty bottles. That should last for a dozen shoot days, with a few more bottles stashed away for domestic consumption on cold winter evenings. The race was on, because country custom had it that at the end of September, the devil would ride out and pee on all the remaining sloes, and that would just not do!

After swimming, a leisurely breakfast took place, making a change from the usual early morning dash. It was porridge followed by eggs and bacon with tomatoes from the greenhouse and marmalade on toast. The dogs had porridge with chunks of cold mutton. Duma and Chui had followed them all into the kitchen. They did their usual thing of rubbing up against Lisette's legs, and once rewarded with a chunks of mutton they ran off with it in their mouths to the privacy of the barn.

After mid-morning, the dogs would be left all day. It was the annual Speech Day and prize-giving at the school. It was de rigueur for all parents to attend and leave afterwards with their children for the exeat weekend with school starting back again on the Tuesday morning. The scheduled guest speaker was the composer Ralph Vaughan Williams. Vaughan Williams had volunteered and served in the Great War initially as a stretcher bearer and later as a commissioned officer in the Artillery which made him partially deaf – not a good thing for a man who was heading towards recognition as England's greatest living composer. His works like 'The Lark Ascending' and adaption of traditional folk and hymn tunes had made him very popular, and for a school that had a strong music department this was a major coup. Regrettably, neither Michael nor Lucy displayed any aptitude for the playing of musical instruments although Joanna and Jennifer Johnson were showing great promise in the violin and cello, respectively. Having done themselves up in their finest, Ash and Lisette departed in the Morris at 10 am and headed for the school.

This was the opportunity the dogs had wanted. Odi had been freed up from duties with Lisette, so she was available to go off with Hunter to meet Minerva. The pair raced through the gap and up to the pool. They waited by the pool, and Minerva having spotted them, came up the channel between the pool and the sea.

"It's been a while," she said. "But you two got there in the end. I'm going to take you somewhere special. Just follow me!"

Tails wagged with excitement as the dogs plunged to the depths of the pool. As Trooper and Rafe had described, it went blurry for a bit, and then they swam up and emerged next to a post twenty yards out to sea from a sandy beach. They looked along the shoreline as they swam in. The land rose, and there were pines and dunes just like at home, but the area was dotted with tents, and to the right, there appeared something of an inlet above which on the higher ground there were masses of large huts with people milling around. There was a bridge across the inlet. There was also an extensive flat area and a flagpole with men marching up and down with a lot of shouting going on. There was a railway line with trains and wagons between the beach and the hutted area. Higher up and further away was a large area of cleared land with hundreds of crosses sticking out of the ground. A dozen men were working there digging. There were a number of flat-topped barrows with long wooden boxes on top of each.

"What is this place?" asked Hunter. "It seems very busy, and I suppose it was nice like home, but with all these people and buildings it doesn't look like fun to me."

Minerva responded. "This place is Étaples and we are in France. I've taken you back in time to June 1918. All those long sheds are hospital wards for wounded soldiers, and this is where they come from the battlefields, which are about fifty miles inland. It is safer here, but the enemy has dropped bombs from aeroplanes killing nurses and their patients. The place with all the crosses is the cemetery because, despite all the efforts of the doctors and nurses, some do not make it. They also train soldiers here to fight before they go to the front, and that is what all the noise is about by the flagpole. I shall leave you here to explore but you must come back in two hours' time. I will meet you back here by the post. Don't worry if you meet any soldiers because they will be nice to you. They like to see the dogs and they give you food, mainly what they call bully beef because there are tins of that all over the place. Quite a lot of the dogs from the town wander up here to meet the soldiers and play with them. The Germans only bomb at night because in the day our pilots will see them and shoot them down. I suggest you go up the beach away from the town. It's a bit quieter up there. I will see you in two hours."

With that, Minerva turned and disappeared beneath the waves.

Hunter and Odi walked along the beach. They spotted a group of men on the edge of the surf about 200 yards ahead. Some were paddling with their trousers rolled up and were bandaged or had their arms in slings. One was being led by another because he had a bandage over his eyes and couldn't see. Two others were in wheelchairs, and some were completely naked in the sea. There were a number of dogs, and the soldiers were throwing sticks into the sea for them to retrieve. One of the dogs was bigger than the rest, but he only had three legs and on his top half he was wearing a soldier's uniform tunic. It fitted him perfectly. The other odd thing was that he was not bringing the sticks back in his mouth like the other dogs but in his front paw that looked like a hand, and he was throwing the sticks himself either for the dogs or straight back to the soldiers who kept shouting to the dog and calling him 'Jackie'. They spoke in an accent that was different from the other soldiers. Odi commented. "That dog looks more like a monkey, but I actually think he is a baboon from Africa. I know that because the mistress once took me to a fair and they had one like that who was dressed up like a clown and he kept doing tricks for everyone."

The dogs joined in the game and had some fun. Odi went and sat by one of the men in the wheelchair. His legs were bandaged, and he had a blanket over them. He was pleased to see Odi and to get attention from her. She allowed him to stroke her and give her chunks of the beef that Minerva had mentioned.

Hunter looked to the edge of the dunes and saw a man and a woman walking side by side. They were both in khaki uniforms. As they came closer, he recognised them. It was Master and Mistress, but they looked a lot younger. He sped over to Odi to alert her and the two bounded up to them.

It was strange because when they got there neither appeared to recognise the dogs, but they did make a fuss of them. The dogs sat beside them as they surveyed the scene.

Lisette said "I'm so glad you brought me here to see this, Ash. It's such a contrast to those wards in the huts. It's so good to see the men happy with hope and some normality restored."

"Indeed," said Ash. "This is something I have been pushing for, and not just for the walking cases. I ordered that a few of the medical orderlies be spared for a couple of hours every day to get the patients down here. It's good for the patients and a welcome change for the orderlies from dealing nonstop with the blood, the mess, the despair and in some cases, the end."

"You are so right on that." said Lisette. "I remember bringing a soldier back from Amiens quite recently. He was one of the South Staffs, but he came from Peterborough where he was a gardener in a park. I think that's not too far from you in Norfolk. He didn't volunteer because he had a wife and two young children. He had lost two of his brothers killed, and two more were wounded. His name was William, William Clark. He was such a nice man, but his lungs were in a very bad way. It was gas, mustard gas, I think. We kept giving him oxygen, but he knew he would not go home. He asked me to write to his wife which I agreed to do. I felt so sorry for him, and I went back to his ward to see him. I held his hand. He went just like that, as if he was waiting for me. Perhaps he thought I was his wife. I cried. They buried him here just a few days ago."

They walked closer to the soldiers. The dogs walked with them. Jackie looked up and walked over to them. He stood up as straight as he could and saluted Ash who returned the salute. "That's amazing, a monkey in military uniform," said Lisette.

Ash explained. "That's Jackie. He would be upset if you called him a monkey. He's a baboon. Believe or not he's officially one of our patients here. Jackie is with the South Africans. They brought him over as a mascot but as he got bigger on all this army food, they enlisted him and had a uniform made to fit. He has served in the trenches all along. Quite useful actually at night on sentry duty with his acute hearing. They trained him to eat with a knife and fork and to salute officers. He was at Delville Wood on the Somme. The South Africans went in with 3,500 men and held it for six days. Only 150 came out along with Jackie. Back in April he was wounded by shrapnel in Belgium. They pleaded with the medics and fortunately one of our surgeons Colonel Woodsend, you might have met him, agreed to operate. The leg was amputated. He was sent to the casualty clearing station all labelled up and then on to here. He's made a magnificent recovery and has been fantastic as a morale booster for the troops."

"Incredible!" said Lisette. "And to think that in the midst of this horror, human kindness came shining through. I love these two dogs here. They seemed to have bonded with us so quickly. If and when we get through all this and can set up home together, we will have to get a pair like this. They may look different, but they are both real working dogs strong and loyal, not like those pampered fluff balls I used to see in Paris."

"I'll go along with that," said Ash. "These would fit in on the estate and that's where we will be heading as soon as this is over. They probably came up from the town. Some get into the camp, but nobody seems to be bothered. The soldiers like them and spoil them. I have a feeling that the end is in sight. Behind Amiens, you should see the tanks, the aircraft and the big guns piling up and all the troops, not just ours. There are Australians, Canadians and even some Americans. Those Australians are really good, strong boys with a bond like brothers. Some of our top brass moan about their discipline and the fact they are always in trouble, but do they fight! And they always achieve what they are asked to do. Their officers are good practical men, not pompous like some of ours. The Australian government refuse to shoot their own men for desertion as we do. When Australians come across our soldiers tied up to a wheel doing what they call 'Field Punishment Number One', the Aussies untie them and let them go, much to the annoyance of some of our officers. The Aussies sort things their way and that seems to work. As for the German prisoners, the ones we treat are glad to be out of it. They talk and they are starting to realise that they are being lied to. Back home ordinary folk are starving. They get bread with sawdust and chalk in it, and they are short on materials so they can't replace guns and aircraft like we do. I think there will be a revolt there sooner or later, but we shall see. I just wonder how many more widows and orphans it will take."

"I've met some of those ANZAC nurses." said Lisette. "They are practical, and not stuffy like some of our old dragons, especially the ones who used to be in the hospitals at home. They seem to think they are a cut above the rest, but with constant work and experience, our VADs and FANYs are every bit as good and some much better. They forget that a lot of our volunteers are much brighter than they are, and the regulars seem to resent that. Those Anzacs are even training some of their nurses to act as anaesthetists. They are very good."

Ash had a few words with the soldiers. Lisette waited further up the beach not wanting to embarrass the nude swimmers, not that soldiers in a state of undress were unacceptable given the nature of her work. The dogs sat with Lisette and when Ash returned, they stayed with them as they walked along the beach until they took the path through the dunes back to camp.

"Bye dogs. Might see you again one day!" said Lisette, unaware of the irony of that remark. She waved and walked on.

Hunter calculated that their time was up, so he and Odi dashed back and swam out to the post. Minerva popped up as they arrived. "Quick, follow me," she said as she dived down with the dogs hot on her tail. The blur returned, and a second or two later they surfaced back at the pool.

"What did you think of that?" asked Minerva.

"It was such a revelation and going back to a time when we were not even born, but it was good to see Master and Mistress and to think that our visit persuaded them to take us all on in the years that followed. It explained a lot and the others will be interested when we tell them."

Minerva said,"I know most of you will be busy on the farm and shoots in the weeks ahead but I will be watching and waiting and when the time is right Nimrod and Kipling can take their turn but there is no rush. When they are ready, I will be here so just pass that on".

Both dogs thanked Minerva and Hunter jumped up and gave her another kiss. They turned and sped off back to the cottage.

Speech day went well. As expected, the Johnson girls got prizes for violin and cello. Lucy got the prize for French. The prizes for sports went to Michael as best boy and Victoria as best girl. Michael's strongest areas were swimming and athletics where he captained both school under thirteens teams. Victoria was a good all-rounder and captained the girls' hockey and netball teams. Simon commented. "We've bred a couple of Olympians there if they carry on at this rate".

Ash responded. "It must be all that countryside living coupled with the fresh food. Those two get on very well and we've noticed that they disappear together at times. Michael keeps asking if Victoria can come swimming with us and the dogs. With temperatures starting to drop there isn't much time left, and I would not like to put the girl off by going in November as we sometimes do. We could do that tomorrow afternoon after church, and she could stay for dinner if that is alright with you. We will see her back safely."

"Please do. She would love the chance to get away from her brothers for a bit. There's no pressure because they won't be going back till Tuesday, so if they need to catch up with prep, they've got all day on Monday. She can come down with Zulu. He adores her and I know he gets on with your pack. Perhaps they will improve his swimming."

Ash had enjoyed listening to Vaughan Williams and noted that the two hymns chosen for the ceremony both used his adapted tunes. He could empathise with anyone who had served at the front, and it was fortuitous that he had made it. He remembered George Butterworth and his 'Banks of Green Willow'. Such talent was lost on the Somme – his body was never found, and there were so many others like the poets Rupert Brooke and Wilfred Owen, brave men who volunteered where the experience of war stimulated their genius but they paid the ultimate sacrifice.

13

Work and play

Zulu was not a fan of church services and that was obvious because he laid next to Odi and slept through the entire service including the Reverend Paddy's impassioned plea for all to attend the harvest festival the following week. This would be followed up with a candlelit harvest supper in the Memorial Hall on the Wednesday evening. The final hymn was a rousing rendition of '*We plough the fields and scatter*', just to rub the message in.

Prior to departure Simon asked if Ash and JJ could attend a meeting at the Hall on the following day as he had a few ideas for the estate that he wanted to go through with them. He indicated that if they had any proposals of their own it would be a useful opportunity to air them openly.

A brisk walk was taken back to the cottage where it was decided that with the advantage of the springboard the lake would be the best option, so they all walked the five minutes to the lake, and on this occasion, the two cats opted to come along too. With Victoria and Zulu as guests, the temptation to show off was too great, so an aerobatic display ensued from the twins. This was followed immediately by the dogs attempting to plunge the furthest after running along the board flat out. Even Lisette and Ash joined in. Lisette performed perfect streamlined dives with hardly any splash, swiftly followed by Ash with his expertise in producing of tidal waves. The dogs goaded Zulu, and he took the plunge. He was a competent swimmer but was totally unable to match the merdogs in their speed or underwater prowess. Victoria matched Lucy in grace and style but lacked Michael's power, speed and distance underwater. Duma and Chui watched bemused from the bank.

After an hour in the water, they all went back to the cottage for ginger beer and a piece of cake. Michael went into the barn and carried out four straw bales, which he placed against the side of the barn. "What are you up to?"asked Victoria.

"I'm complying with the law of the land," he responded.

Victoria stared quizzically. Michael went back into the barn and produced a longbow with a sheaf of arrows and a target of painted cardboard, which he attached to the bales.

He explained. "Edward III decreed in 1363 that we should all practise archery on Sundays and holidays. Other sports were banned. It's more important than going to church."

The bow was quite powerful with a thirty-pound pull. Michael continued. "Dad got one of the estate carpenters to make it for me. He crafted it from a yew branch. He does it as a hobby and he is very good. Dad has one with a sixty-pound pull, and that's a bit of a beast, but that's nothing compared to the bows that King Edward's archers were using. They were twice as powerful as that, but with all that practice, they ended up with deformed shoulders and arms. In battle, they were superb, and that was all that really mattered."

He then gave Victoria a lesson in archery after fitting her up with a wrist protector to stop the string from cutting in. They started at ten yards and gradually moved back. Victoria was excited to do something new. Lucy joined in and was reasonably proficient.

Eventually, Michael took it back to thirty yards and put several arrows quite close to the bull's eye.

He explained. "It's all a matter of time and practice. Eventually, the bow becomes an extension of your body. I don't aim now like I used to. I just look at the target with both eyes open, draw back and 'will' the arrow to the centre. I know it's not nice, but sometimes when I am about to release the arrow, I say the name of someone who has upset me or a nasty person I have read about and that seems to help."

At 5 pm, dinner was served. All the exercise had produced good appetites, but there was more than plenty, so all the dogs and cats enjoyed their allocation too.

By 7pm it was starting to get dark. Ash intimated that he should be taking Victoria back. Michael pleaded that he could escort her. "It's not a problem. It's only ten minutes and I've done it on my own loads of times and if the dogs come, she will be more than safe. You know what they are like with strangers."

"So be it," said Ash. "But if you are not back in thirty minutes sharp, I'll be coming for you".

Both Victoria and Michael smiled in contentment. Time alone was something they treasured.

On the following day, Lisette allowed the twins to lie in until 8 am, then they were up and off with all the dogs for a dip in the sea. Lisette prepared breakfast and Ash talked with her about an idea he had for the estate. Lisette's knowledge of the financial aspects was handy because she dealt with a lot of the estate's bills and arranged payment.

After breakfast, Ash drove off in the truck for the scheduled meeting at the Hall. The twins did a bit of homework for a couple of hours then took off for a walk in the woods with the dogs. Odi would remain with Lisette. They told her they were going to the castle keep on the far western side of the estate just above the salt marsh and would walk back along the beach.

Ash arrived at the Hall and met JJ on the front lawn. Amrik came out and bade them enter. They went to the library where Simon was sat at the smaller table they used for more intimate meetings. He had a file of paperwork in front of him. Coffees were served. Simon was pleased to report that Victoria had spent a splendid afternoon at the cottage and had asked if any Christmas gift could include a longbow. Ash agreed to sort it. JJ spoke of his daughters and their career options. They were now aged sixteen and nearly eighteen. Both were doing well academically. They were looking at medicine and Joanna the eldest with a passion for horses had indicated veterinary medicine. JJ felt that both would make the grade for acceptance at appropriate medical schools.

With coffee out of the way, the time had come for the main business. Simon began by outlining the current situation. Despite the national picture that remained gloomy due to the great depression, the farm side of the business was doing well. It was not making huge profits, but was holding its own. There was still a lot of money slushing around with the upper echelons of society and that was something he felt they could tap into. Those with something new and attractive to offer would benefit. He was of the view that whilst prices were depressed, this was the right time to invest in terms of development. He continued and mentioned that on his trips to London he had met up with Geoffrey de Havilland who was at the forefront of aviation design and development. De Haviland had produced bombers in the Great War and was now looking to expand into in the civilian market. Simon had been taking lessons in flying for several years and was a qualified competent pilot. His flying had been confined to membership of the Norfolk and Norwich Aero Club at Mousehold Heath near Norwich where he had a part share of a Gipsy Moth biplane.

"The aviation leisure side of things is getting big. Those with money are buying aircraft, joining clubs and in a few years from now, will be using aircraft to go on holiday and business trips. We are halfway between Sandringham and Norwich, so I propose that we lay out an airfield with two 1,000-yard grass runways with a hangar, tower, club room and restaurant. The estate will purchase a Gipsy Moth and possibly one of the new Tiger Moths that de Havilland is producing. It would be ideal on the plateau between the two valleys at the southern end of the estate. I also propose that we build ten luxury chalets on the eastern side of the lake next to the boathouse. We will be able to offer lake and sea fishing, a peaceful exclusive setting, shooting, riding and fine dining with conference facilities. The farming side of the estate will continue uninterrupted, but we need to move with the times to ensure our income keeps up in the years ahead, so we need to move now. What do you think?" asked Simon.

"Sounds visionary," said JJ. "But where are we going to get the money for this?"

Simon responded. "This is strictly between us. Agreed?"

Ash and JJ nodded.

"Helen's father is not getting any younger. He has made a lot of money with his tea and coffee plantation, and he doesn't want the efforts of his enterprise filched by this or any other government, so he has released a large sum that will not be liable for tax if he lives a few more years, as I am sure he will." Simon responded.

"Well, that's fortuitous and I think what you propose is sound. My only reservation is the type of people who end up in these chalets. We don't want these Bullingdon toffs wrecking the place and our reputation." said JJ.

Ash interjected. "That's simply done. We merely state from the outset that single-sex parties will not be accommodated. I am mindful that it's not just the testosterone brigade. I remember the war and the outrageous activities of the munitionettes. As a result of those ladies, we ended up with our licensing laws, watered-down beer and they started recruiting policewomen to keep them under control. Whilst we might worry about getting the wrong types, the price should ensure that they will stay away and the numbers remain modest. I hear that over in Skegness, Billy Butlin has persuaded the Earl of Scarborough to lease him land and he has put in a massive fun fair with all sorts of contraptions and even a zoo. It's been running for about four or five years now. The latest is that he wants to expand to make it into a huge holiday camp. I say good luck to him but from what I hear he's a bit of a rough one. He carries a cutthroat razor. There are some shady characters in the fun fair game with quite a bit of competition for that sort of business but it's not the sort of thing we want. From a purely selfish perspective I'm glad the chalets will be on the boathouse side of the lake as the pines and dunes are pristine. The preservation of that side will benefit those seeking peace and natural tranquillity, providing set walking routes are identified and clearly marked."

Simon couldn't resist coming back on that. "Well, Ash, at least your side of the lake which serves as a communal outside bathroom for your family, and mine as of yesterday, will be preserved but I think it is time that we moved you on from the Stone Age. You can forget about the water tower. I intend to have you put on mains gas and water, and that will be an extension from the chalets. We also need to ensure that the track from the village and harbour up to the boathouse is upgraded to a road. And the same standard will apply to the rest of the houses on the estate including Boynton's. His cottage is on the route up to the airfield and that will need a bit of an upgrade although I'm not suggesting highway quality. An all-weather estate track will suffice. Can I assume that you are both in agreement?"

Both nodded.

Simon continued "Do either of you have any suggestions? I don't have the monopoly on new ideas. Why don't we take a short break? We have been at it for a couple of hours now, and I think a Jameson's has been well earned."

Simon poured out three large whiskies.

They took a ten-minute break. Ash was thinking about his conversation with Lisette. His greatest strength as a manager was that he was not crisis led. Whilst most people thought a few days or weeks ahead, Ash's analytical mind was always thinking years ahead, constantly planning, and testing his ideas in conversation with experienced and knowledgeable individuals before putting things forward. As business resumed Ash said. "There is one area where we could save money and get a better service."

"Where's that?" asked Simon.

"We have at peak times well in excess of 2,000 head of livestock as well as twenty horses and the periodic needs in respect of our deer herd and game birds. Our veterinary bills including call-out charges and prescription medicines could more than pay for a veterinary surgery with a couple of vets in our own right. If we established our own in-house practice, any callouts would be quicker. A rapid response can mean things might get better before they get worse. Medicines would be cheaper by buying direct without the markup, and if matters progress, we could even provide a small animal practice for the villages. As you know we host the household cavalry for a camp by the beach every year for a week. I have been speaking to their veterinary officer, a major who is coming up to the end of his twenty-two years of contracted service and he is looking for something. He has a lot of experience with horses and livestock as he comes from a farming family and every year, he used to spend quite a bit of leave time at his parent's farm helping out. His wife is a nurse, and he has just one son who is over at Cambridge studying veterinary medicine. I'm also mindful of what Julian's Joanna wants to do in a year's time when she finishes at school. If we took him on to start things up, I think we have the potential for a good future."

"My God," said Simon. "I wish I'd thought of that. I'm angry with myself for missing it. I know we have a good relationship with our vet, but he is ten miles away and he's not cheap. We always have to compete with demands from other farms and dogs and cats. Julian, what's your view?"

JJ responded. "I can think of no reason not to go ahead. We will have to build a reasonable house integrated with a surgery and probably a couple of semis to cater for staff expansion but that could be accomplished in a few months. That would probably be best somewhere opposite the church as most of our livestock is north of the main road and it would be close to the village."

Simon concluded. "Right. We will do it. Can you, Ash, make the approach to the major? And if things are to proceed, can you, JJ, initiate any building works while we get on with the other matters? Next Saturday is the first shoot day of the season. As you know for the first day, we usually run it on a commercial basis with paying guests. We have five guns booked via the agency and I have invited Geoffrey de Havilland to pick his brains on the airfield. He will fly into Norwich on Friday and will stay here possibly for two nights. I have also invited Captain Van Neck the chief constable. I spoke to him about Snodgrass. They have found him a job at police headquarters dealing with found property, and we are getting a younger man, a PC Carter with a reputation for getting things sorted. He comes from a farming background so that should help. By the way we have a lady coming to join in your picking-up team for the day Ash. She is the secretary of the Gundog Field Trials Society. She's a Miss Fawcett – bit of an old battleaxe from what I hear. I know you regard these types as a bit odd, but please treat her gently."

"Thanks, Simon," said Ash. "You've certainly made my day with the news about Snodgrass. As for Miss Fawcett, I'll be polite, but as you know picking up for real is very different from field trials stuff."

It was twelve noon. There was a knock at the door. Amrik entered with a footman. They brought in trays of tasty morsels for lunch with a fine chilled Chablis that was relished by the three comrades and brothers-in-arms of the Spelthorpe Company.

On the following Friday afternoon, Simon collected Geoffrey de Havilland from the Norwich airfield. He had flown in one of his new Tiger Moth biplanes that was earmarked for the Royal Air Force as a basic trainer. They went to the Hall and after settling his guest in Simon took him up to the site planned for the airfield. The two perpendicular runways at 1,000 yards were more than adequate with minimal levelling and there was potential to add another 300 yards to each if required at some stage in the future. A Gipsy Moth would be ideal to start with. It was after all the plane that made Amy Johnson a household name two years earlier when she flew one all the way to Australia. Geoffrey intimated that he was working on a new, fast, covered twin-engine bi plane that would take up to eight passengers. The airfield would be able to cater for that adequately should visitors to the estate want to fly in. Pleasantly reassured, Simon took Geoffrey back to the Hall. Geoffrey had served in the Royal Flying Corps in the war, so they had tales to tell over a convivial dinner to which JJ and his wife had been invited. After dinner, the gentlemen retired to the billiard room with brandy and cigars.

14

Shooting bloomers

On the following day Ash and Lisette were up early. They all had a quick swim in the lake as the sun came up. After breakfast they both left for the Hall with all the dogs in the back of the truck. Lisette was dressed to act as co-hostess and would be helping Helen to welcome the guests and oversee the shoot lunch.

Ash had a collar and tie but wore his waxed Barbour thornproof that was ideal for pushing through undergrowth. It had large poachers' pockets for his game carriers, truncheon priest and other kit. He would be running the picking-up team and would have four other pickers plus Miss Gertrude Fawcett. JJ would run the day allocating stand numbers to Simon and the seven other guests. These would be drawn by lot, and after each drive, the gun would move up two places running from right to left to ensure that all got a chance to be where most of the action was to be. JJ would tow the trailer in which the guns would be seated and would indicate where they should stand – normally in a line with twenty yards between each.

Six game drives were planned for the day with four before lunch and two afterwards. Several experienced farmhands were allocated to act as paid loaders if that was required, but Geoffrey and the chief constable elected to load themselves.

Boynton would direct the actual drives with his two underkeepers. They were dressed in their best tweeds because that was the tradition. Likewise, the loaders would normally carry up to 150 cartridges for each drive. A dozen beaters from the farm and village would be acting under the instruction of the keepers, and they were suitably attired for pushing through cover crops and undergrowth in the woods as they flushed the game and drove it forward towards the guns. Most had brought a springer spaniel along with them to help flush the game.

All assembled at the front of the hall with Amrik and his staff offering drinks to the guns. Ash spotted Gertrude Fawcett straight away. She was a somewhat oversized lady who had forced herself into her undersized tweeds in the vain hope that it would improve matters. She had a springer spaniel and a black Labrador, both of which were held on tight leads. Gertrude was very unsettled when the other picking-up dogs, all off lead, attempted to introduce themselves by the customary mutual sniffing of the nether regions. Nimrod in particular, an ardent bum sniffer, thrust his nose up Miss Fawcett's skirt to follow up. He didn't remain long as she slammed her thighs together. Ash said, "Nimrod. Behave!"

Ash introduced himself and said, "I see you have an each-way bet today, having brought one of each," He gestured towards her dogs. "I was always told that with a Labrador you get a dog that is half-trained from the start but with a Springer you get one that is half-trained at the end!"

Gertrude responded, "These are both Field trial champions!"

"That's good, I'll be interested to see how they perform," said Ash. Gertrude looked across to see Odi and Hunter sitting side by side. "What is that sheepdog thing doing here?"

"That's Odi," said Ash. "She is not only a superb picking-up dog, but she understands and can count in both English and French. She's bilingual".

"I don't believe it," said Gertrude. "Absolutely ridiculous – a sheepdog. Well, I never!"

Ash quietly said, "Odi. Cherche moi mes gants. Ils sont dans le camion." With that Odi jumped into the cab of the truck and returned seconds later with Ash's gloves.

Ash continued. "Well, there you have it. Perhaps you might consider a bilingual category in your field trials. We get French guests here on occasions, what with the Entente Cordiale and all that, and it works both ways because my Labradors help out when we are lambing. Anyway, you will be in the truck cab with me. The others and their dogs will be in the back and in the second truck. Your dogs can go with them if you want. I'll get one of the pickers to look after them or you can have them with you in the front."

Miss Fawcett indicated that they would go with her in the cab. They jumped in readily enough, but dear Gertrude needed a very large shoehorn as her mammoth backside squeezed its way in. *Fawcett by name, force it by nature*, thought Ash.

At 9 am, they set off and headed for the top of the valley near the southwestern end of the estate. The guns were lined up along the brook that ran through the valley. It was a little boggy in the valley and wooden platforms made of packing crates had been placed at twenty-yard intervals. The birds would be driven from the wood to fly across the valley onto a mix of wood and scrub on the other side. Ash explained to Gertrude. "I'll have you at the front in the middle so you should get plenty of action. There will be one picker to your right sixty yards further down and I'll be to your left. Dogs must not go in front of the guns during the drive unless we have a wounded runner. They understand that.

Birds falling behind the guns may be collected but wounded birds are the priority. The rest of the pickers-up are behind on the plateau, and they will work forward when the shooting stops on the long whistle. Two short bursts of the whistle will start the drive."

Ash's first line was fifty yards behind the guns and the second line on the plateau was 150 yards back. Similar instructions had been given to the guns.

Merdogs at the ready

Ash walked up the valley with his team of merdogs. He said nothing to them. They knew what to do. Ash's firm belief was that dogs learnt by watching at an early age, so his instructions were minimal. The dogs would see more than he did, and their sense of smell would identify things like of a blood trail in the air, and that would tell them whether it was worth going back to look. Often in the past a dog would turn and disappear only to come back with a wounded bird that had to be dispatched. The ongoing problem was that some guns did not shoot well or would attempt the impossible with higher birds. It was something Ash would like to change, and he did persuade Simon that inexperienced shooters should be offered some clay pigeon practice with an underkeeper on the eve of the shoot. Some took that up. Loaders were encouraged to advise inexperienced guns on the day. Realistically given the strong lobby for tradition it was not something that would change overnight, but it was something that Spelthorpe could lead on. That was why Ash preferred pigeon shooting alone, where he would only take what was a viable shot and he rarely missed. Pheasant shooting was not for him.

The dogs had settled in and chosen their positions. Rafe did the oddest of things and on this day, he went right up the valley with Trooper in tow, but his judgement was rarely wrong. Ash would watch him sniffing, and thinking, sensing the wind and listening to the pheasant noise on the other side of the valley. Nimrod and Kipling went up the valley about 50 yards. Odi and Hunter remained with Ash and waited for any specific instructions.

The two whistles sounded. Miss Fawcett shouted up to Ash. "Just watch this! I'll show you how it's done." Ash smiled back politely and waved noting that both of Gertrude's dogs remained on the lead. About a minute later the birds started coming – a mix of pheasant and partridge slowly at first but increasing in numbers in a spectacular display. Ash saw that on leaving the wood opposite, many of the birds were flying across and up the valley, so Rafe was right yet again. Shots were fired and birds started dropping. Miss Fawcett was letting her dogs off the lead when she spotted a bird and then started flailing her arms in the air like a convulsing semaphore pole. She kept whistling and shouting and whilst concentrating on one bird and one dog, she missed the others and a wounded pheasant running in front of the guns. Ash sent Hunter for that. He was back in seconds. Odi darted in and brought back a couple of partridges in one go and all this time Gertrude was flailing away attempting to direct her robotic dog. Eventually, it returned with a pheasant, but not the one she had sent it for. Hunter spotted that and grabbed it and ran back. Up the valley the other merdogs were doing their job working as a team and covering if one dog was busy or going back on a trail. Trooper was up to his usual trick of bringing up to four partridges back at a time. He liked to show off. The dogs worked in an uncompetitive way as if choreographed by instinct and experience to bring back birds as quickly as possible and ran back to Ash with them if dispatching was required.

After some ten minutes, the long whistle sounded, and Ash started walking up towards Rafe picking up the odd bird as he walked and collecting them from the neat piles that the dogs had created. The pickers at the rear started working forwards. "Oh, I don't do that," bellowed Gertrude. "I make my dogs collect everything. I think I did rather well there. My dogs got four birds. How did you get on?"

Ash said nothing but pointed to a pile of some twenty-five where he had been standing.

A few minutes later, Ash returned from up the valley carrying some twenty birds back from the far end that Rafe and Trooper had collected. The guns and loaders were chatting and had clearly had a good first drive although amused eyes were fixed on Miss Fawcett, who was standing balanced on a rock in the stream screaming abuse at her two dogs, who in a state of full revolt, were devouring a pheasant on the other side. Her arm signals became ever more frantic as she attempted to maintain balance, and then the rest of her body was cavorting backwards and forwards in an extreme effort to stay upright. Suddenly the tight-fitting tweed skirt could no longer take the strain as it burst apart and fell away, exposing a voluminous pair of lacy white bloomers. Gertrude suddenly toppled forward into the middle of the stream with an enormous splash and a roaring scream. Her bloomers were drenched and became translucent from the water, exposing a gigantic set of pink buttocks. Gertrude groaned like a beached tweed whale, blocking the stream with the water damming up against her. The guns erupted in explosive laughter and tempting though it was to join in, Ash did not want the stream blocked, so he merely went forward taking off his Barbour to conceal the display. He got her up and escorted her back to the truck. Another picker took charge of her dogs.

It was fortunate that the next drive was further down the valley, and Ash was able to make a short detour to deposit Miss Fawcett at the Hall, placing her in the care of Lisette. He whispered to her, "I'll tell you about it later."

He borrowed one of Simon's Barbours and resumed his responsibilities in his picking-up role. On the next three game drives, free of Miss Fawcett, Ash resumed his normal position working at the back, sweeping up with his team whilst the other pickers were sent forward as they were operating with fewer dogs.

The rest of the day went well. At lunchtime the guns went back to the Hall. Miss Fawcett had decided to take her leave. Lisette had managed to create a temporary skirt on a sowing machine using canvas from an old tent. Ash went down to the village pub. It was important that he attend to preserve the 'espirit de corps' amongst the shoot workers rather than lunch with the earl and guests despite being invited.

The usual arrangements had been made for a hot meal and a pint for the beaters and pickers. The pub was owned by the estate but tenanted to a jovial former navy chief stoker who was glad of the extra business. Most of the dogs were admitted. Boynton and his underkeepers came too. It was a glorious fug of a meaty stew and dumplings, best bitter, tobacco smoke and steaming dogs wet from the stream. The assembly erupted in raucous laughter as Ash related the tale of Miss Fawcett's translucent bloomers.

The twins arrived back at the Hall at 2 pm. Lisette had a change of clothes for them, and they joined up with their father to work the dogs for the last two drives. Rafe and Trooper went with the master. Michael took Nimrod and Kipling. Odi and Hunter went with Lucy.

Both had done this for many years and were very experienced.

The day ended at 4pm. The day's tally was 352 pheasants and 153 partridges, which was compatible with the number the paying guests had expected. Getting the numbers right was a skill Boynton excelled at, and he normally got it spot on. The chief constable had offered to take Geoffrey de Havilland back to Norwich and from there it would only be an hour for the flight back home in his Gipsy Moth in good daylight.

15

Jambo msichana, Jambo mbwa (Hello miss, Hello dogs)

Sunday 2nd October 1932

Following on from the previous Sunday Simon had decided to invite the whole family up for a late Sunday lunch following a spot of riding for the twins. To do things the other way around was asking for trouble.

Sunday morning went as usual. There was a swim in the lake followed by breakfast. Given that the appointment at the Hall followed church and the harvest festival, it was decided that all the dogs should remain at the cottage for the rest of the day. Ash collected a basket of vegetables from the garden, and they all walked the mile and a half up to the church.

Departure for the day presented the dogs with an opportunity. It was the turn of Nimrod and Kipling to go with Minerva. They dashed up to the pool and waited. Within a few minutes she appeared, having swum up the channel from the open sea.

"Looks like you managed it in the end, but I am going to ensure that your patience is rewarded. We are going somewhere special, and I think you will like it. Just follow me down and all will be revealed," said Minerva.

The dogs dived down and surfaced a few seconds later with Minerva by their side. They swam in the few yards to where the water was about a foot deep. The water was warm and fish with black tips to their dorsal fins kept swimming past zig zagging on the edge of the surf.

"What are these strange fish?" asked Nimrod.

"They are sharks, baby black tip sharks and this is their nursery where they are safe and out of the way of larger sharks who might want to eat them. They will grow to almost eight feet long as adults but even then, although curious, they are usually harmless, not like the big tiger sharks and great whites that cruise beyond the edge of the reef way out there where you see the waves breaking. We won't be going out there. The only sharks to worry about here are the bull sharks. They will snap at anything in the shallows, but what makes them more dangerous is that they swim for miles and miles from the sea up the rivers. It's worse still because the rivers are full of Nile crocodiles, and they will attack anything that comes close. But generally, you will be safe in the lagoon and that is where we are now," explained Minerva.

Kipling said, "I like this place with this white sand. What are those trees all along higher up the beach?"

Minerva responded. "They are coconut palms. They are very useful trees. The trunk is used to build huts and houses. The leaves are used for roofs and can be woven to make baskets and fish traps. The large green fruits have a nut inside that you can eat and are full of clear liquid you can drink. It is very pure and free of anything that can harm you and has a balance of salts and sugars that is sometimes used as a transfusion to replace body fluids in somebody who is ill. The hair around the nuts can be used for brushes and to make mats. It's a wonderful tree.

The tree gives you shade against the hot tropical sun but before you go underneath make sure there are no nuts above you because every year people get killed when the heavy fruits drop down on them. When the nuts fall sometimes, they roll into the sea. The nut is a seed. They drift in the current, sometimes for hundreds of miles, and when they get washed up a new tree grows in the sand. That is useful because the roots of the tree go down for fresh water and that stops the sand from getting washed away. I think we will stay here on the edge, although I can see a man wearing a turban with a young girl up there sitting but not right under the trees."

Nimrod gazed across at the man. "He looks a bit like Amrik to me but a lot younger."

The girl who was about nine years old came running down the beach when she saw the dogs. The man stayed in the shade. Both dogs wagged their tails to show the girl they were friendly.

"Jambo mbwa," said the girl as she got close. She stroked the dogs.

"It might help if you speak in English rather than Swahili," said Minerva. "The dogs only understand English, but your Swahili is excellent. Have you been speaking it long?"

"About six months since I got here," she said. "The African houseboys and girls are teaching me. The young man up the beach is Amrik. He is our head houseboy, but he came with us from India. He is learning Swahili too. It's the language they all speak along the coast. We live here about five miles up that way," she pointed, " just outside place called Mombasa which has a big harbour. I don't go to school because my mother is teaching me. My father wants us to live at a place called Nairobi. That's about three hundred miles away in the high country."

"Why is that?" asked Minerva.

"We like it here, but it is too hot, and where there is fresh water and wet there is malaria. It is better to be close to the beach. My father grows tea and coffee. He grows a lot in India, but he wants to start doing it here and he thinks that close to Nairobi will be a good place. We went up there a few weeks ago on the train. It took ages and when you get there it's just loads of railway lines and trucks and a lot of building going on. When you look out of the window on the train you see elephants and giraffes and lots of different animals. There are some nasty ones too. The railway has only been finished about a year. To build it, they brought lots of men over from India, and now their families are coming too, but when they were building the railway at a place called Tsavo the lions kept eating all the railway workers. There were two lions that were very bad. They would go in tents and drag men out in the night and would get through the fences around the camps. Some say they ate more than a hundred people. They became quite famous these man-eaters of Tsavo. People were so frightened they didn't want to work there, and work almost stopped so they got a hunter, and he shot the lions, but it wasn't easy because the lions nearly got him too."

At that moment a troop of monkeys emerged from the edge of the coconut palms.

"Those vervet monkeys are everywhere," said the girl. "You have to be careful because they steal things."

"How do you recognise and name the monkeys?" asked Minerva. "They all look the same to me."

"That's easy," said the girl. "Look at the back end. You'll see they have got bright blue balls. We call them the blue balls monkeys but that's just the boys. That's what I like about this place, but I'm not frightened but you do have to be careful especially at night. If you make a noise most animals will stay away, but you should carry a torch because of the night adders that don't move until you step on one. We have two mongooses at home, and they keep the snakes away. I hate the puff adders. They are fat and strike like lightning, so you have to be careful where you walk especially around rocky places. All the people here, like in India, go around in bare feet and hundreds get killed every year. I think that's why they have so many children. They tell me the hippopotamus is the most dangerous animal in Africa but that is because they react if you get between them and the water. In the water they feel safe, so they are not a problem.

"I'm Minerva and this is Nimrod and Kipling. What is your name?" asked Minerva.

"I'm Helen," responded the girl. "I like the name Nimrod. That's a good strong name. I shall remember that. Nimrod and Kipling!" With that she stroked the dogs and paddled in the surf beside them as she threw lumps of driftwood for them to retrieve.

They played for about half an hour then there was a shout from Amrik.

"I have to go now," said Helen. "It was good to meet you all, but I doubt if they will believe me when I say I met a real mermaid." Helen turned and walked up the beach.

The dogs and Minerva stayed for another half an hour but as the sun rose higher in the sky it got hotter and hotter. "Time we were off." said Minerva. They dived under the surface only to emerge seconds later in the colder waters of north Norfolk.

"I know you are busy now and the days are getting shorter, and the water colder so I may not see you for a while," said Minerva. "But we will get back together again quite soon I hope".

Kipling spoke. "Thank you, Minerva. That was fantastic, and the other merdogs will be very jealous when we tell them where we have been. We will keep up the swimming as much as we can. See you soon".

With that, the dogs trotted back along the sand to the cottage. The others were jealous when they heard the story but as Kipling pointed out, they did have to wait the longest.

The church was packed which was only to be expected in a community with a deep attachment to the land. Such feelings went back thousands of years long before Jesus stuck his head above the parapet. Most folks were what you would call 'God fearing' and saw the Almighty as a creator and provider. That included Amrik and his wife so in that sense, they were all of one faith, with Christianity merely representing a way of doing things in this part of the world in a way that had become very English over the centuries. The harvest festival was possibly the most important day for this gathering of farming folk and an opportunity to express thanks for the sun, rain, plants and creatures on which they all depended.

Even Boynton who was usually absent from Sunday services turned up with a couple of pheasants. In addition to the wide selection of homegrown produce there was a special harvest loaf in the shape of a sheaf of wheat. The service was also attended by a tethered Suffolk ram, a Tamworth pig and one of the brown polls from the dairy herd. In all there was a splendid display that enhanced the thanksgiving. Amos brought along two of his six border collies.

At the end of the day all the produce would go up to the local cottage hospital at the far end of the village and to anyone identified as needy within the local area.

Simon and Ash managed to get away just after 1 pm. All the kids of both families went down to the stables where the two Johnson sisters supervised. They rode two of the Suffolk Punches, and the others were sorted by size and ability between the Welsh mountain ponies and the cobs. Their route would take them down past the cottage along the edge of the pines to the castle keep and back along the sands with confidence-building gallops on the edge of the surf – a seven-mile trek in all. That would afford Simon, Ash and their ladies a couple of hours of respite for pre-dinner drinks, nibbles and relaxation in the orangery which overlooked the terrace and lake. Amrik served up, then left them alone. Simon outlined the feedback from the guns on the previous day. The shooting had been top class, and he had thanked Boynton for getting things spot on as ever. The guests had also commented that despite the additional noise, they had enjoyed the cabaret comedy act thrown in by Miss Fawcett. Ash related the tale in full including her comments about Odi, the bilingual retrieving sheep dog, and the exploding skirt and bloomers. By the end Helen and Lisette had an attack of uncontrollable giggles that endured for several minutes. Simon congratulated Ash on his diplomacy in dealing with the situation. Ash explained that given enough rope, people would usually hang themselves, and that was precisely what had happened yesterday. His view was that a good handler would work with his or her dogs recognising that the dogs had qualities that mere humans lacked and to convert a dog into something of a robot purely to satisfy one's own ego, would, in time, strip those qualities away. Simon agreed, stating that both Geoffrey and the Chief Constable had commented on the remarkable performance of Ash's team without any shouting or wild flailing signals. Helen came in at that point. "You two do seem to have such a special way with those dogs of yours. Victoria never stopped talking about how they were diving off the springboard then submerging like a bob of seals. I don't know how you manage to teach them to do that, even Odi was getting stuck in".

"Funny you should say that, "said Lisette. "I first noticed it when I came back with the children from Folkestone for the start of term. When I mentioned it to Ash, he said in jest that they had probably met a mermaid on the beach but the following day at church Odi was totally fixed on that stained-glass window with the mermaid. It was uncanny. She was staring at it for a full hour".

"You've got me now," said Helen. "I've never mentioned it before, and I don't want you sending me off to the funny farm, but when I was in Kenya all those years ago, I was about nine and I was on the beach with Amrik watching over me from a distance and I came across two dogs with a mermaid. We had a chat, and she understood the Swahili I was learning. The dogs were the spitting image of your two youngest dogs, and I distinctly remember the names Nimrod and Kipling – not the sort of names you would forget. We played retrieving sticks in the surf for quite a time before I left. When I got home, I told my mother, and she told me not to be so stupid".

"That's really odd." said Lisette. "Ash do you remember the beach at Etaples in the war when we saw the soldiers playing with that baboon in uniform and those two dogs came up to us? They were the spitting image of Hunter and Odi and it was as if they knew us right from the start."

"I remember it well," said Ash. "It's uncanny, and even more so after what Helen has come out with. There's so much we just don't understand. I get those funny feelings when on a clear night I look up and see all those stars and what I am seeing is what happened hundreds of years ago. But there again we have just come from church where we are supposed to believe that a guy changed water into wine, walked on water, fed thousands with five loaves and two fishes and after he was killed came back to life three days later, walked around for a bit appearing in locked rooms and then took off into space. Thinking back, a month ago when we were out fishing it was Rafe who directed us to where the fish were, and we caught loads. That was the sort of stunt that Jesus pulled off. I can't work it all out so we will just have to accept that our dogs may very, very possibly have discovered time travel, but we will just have to keep it secret, or we'll all be joining Helen in the funny farm".

Simon relayed his conversation with Geoffrey about the

airfield so that was a new venture they could all get involved with. JJ would be moving ahead on that. Simon had placed an order for a new Gipsy Moth biplane. The next couple of months would be busy. The cattle and pigs had gleaned over the cereal fields and orchard so ploughing was imminent and in a month the Guy Fawkes parade would be upon them.

At 4.30pm the children came back. Michael was soaked, having fallen in the surf when his horse stumbled slightly whilst racing Victoria. Four of the dogs had joined them for the horse ride when they passed the cottage leaving Nimrod and Kipling on guard but other than that all was fine. Neither Ash nor Simon seemed the least concerned by the fall. Both believed that controlled exposure to risk was essential to survival and at least he had demonstrated how to tumble without injury. Importantly the horse was fine.

The late lunch was superb – finest rib of beef washed down with an excellent claret followed by blackberry crumble with clotted cream and a fine cognac for the finale. All in all, it had been an excellent day. As darkness fell, they returned to the cottage.

16

Gunpowder, Treason and Plot

October-November 1932

October on the estate followed the usual pattern. Ploughing was underway. The leaves on the trees were starting to turn to a golden brown. Trees for felling and coppicing in the month ahead had been selected and a thousand large whips were earmarked to be dug up as bare-root trees for replanting over November. About 500 lambs and a hundred two-year red poll cattle had gone off to market and slaughter, with others including some of the pigs dealt with locally at the small estate slaughterhouse for domestic needs and sale by the estate shop which included a butchery. The rams had done their duty, so all was set up for the next season. Ash had contacted Major Rufus De Lisle of the Royal Army Veterinary Corps and following a visit and meeting with Earl Simon, Ash and JJ, he had agreed to take up a position on the estate in the spring when he left the army. The Corps was slimming down considerably from its peak in the Great War with the onset of peace. There was finally a recognition that horses and modern warfare do not mix well, and they were being replaced by mechanisation and the use tracked vehicles in rough country. The army and air force still used dogs for guard duties. Rufus had intimated that his son Jeremy would be graduating in less than a year and had an interest in joining if a second position was made available to him. He asked if Jeremy could come up for a look around.

Simon said. "That will be absolutely fine. Perhaps he could come here on a Sunday and Joanna could show him round the place. I know she wants to train to be vet when she finishes at school in June so they will have something to talk about. Does Jeremy ride?"

"Indeed, he does." said Rufus.

"Well, that settles it then, if that's all right with you JJ? I 'd like the chance to meet him too." said Simon.

Simon told them he had been approached by the Norfolk foxhounds yet again about holding a meet on his estate. The earl's view was unchanged.

"I won't have those drunken horsey hooligans on my land wrecking the place. They seem to think they have God given right to do as they please and you end up with damage all over the place just for one bloody fox. They call it part of the English tradition, but I can see nothing sporting about a mass of hounds chasing one fox for miles and ripping it apart. We have a few, the right number, and if things get out of hand Boynton deals with it, quickly, quietly and efficiently. That's the way it's going to stay so that's what I told them. I might have lost a few friends, but true friends help, and this lot are all for themselves".

Ash and JJ nodded in agreement.

Simon asked if things were lined up on Ash's side for the November fifth bonfire party.

"Yes, all in hand, Simon. The foresters have done their bit. If the weather holds, we will have a good evening."

The dogs had been busy with the shooting season in full swing. There had been four sold days and two guest days in the month. A special guest day was scheduled for late November. They had not had the opportunity to meet up with Minerva for any length of time. As October drew to a close, night-time temperatures were palpably cooler although Ash's tough clan were still dipping in the lake and the sea, albeit for shorter periods. The cold never worried the dogs, although both the dogs and cats were now gravitating to the front of the Aga in the evenings.

The fifth of November was always a special day on the Spelthorpe estate. It would normally coincide with school half terms so all the children of the estate and village could attend as well as those undergoing private education. This year it fell on a Saturday, but the actual day was critical, and it was never a case of moving it to the nearest weekend. The history was important and included the years following Guy Fawke's attempt to blow up the king and parliament simultaneously. James I had remained overtly protestant despite his late mother Mary Queen of Scots being a catholic, at least until Good Queen Bess chopped her head off for treason. The same could not be said of subsequent kings who were tainted with Catholicism by marriage or were closet Catholics themselves. For the next half century only Oliver Cromwell and his parliamentarians had stood apart. Cromwell was a man of East Anglia, a farmer, raised at Huntingdon and later living in Ely. With his 'troop of horse' he formed the cornerstone of the Eastern Association of the neighbouring East Anglia counties. He rose with brilliant generalship to lead the Parliamentary army to victory in the civil war. Only King's Lynn and Lincoln stood apart, but they were swiftly dealt with. During the war and restoration Spelthorpe had maintained a low profile like so many others, but fully supported the invasion by William of Orange also on the fifth November in 1688. The Glorious Revolution that ensued secured Spelthorpe's survival.

Whilst the historic significance remained, the evening procession and bonfire was retained as the one time in the year when everyone could let their hair down. It was the one day when first names were the order of the day regardless of any position or rank on the understanding that on the following day the usual rules of etiquette and respect applied.

Although in some quarters, offence might be taken, this was an event to which all regardless of religious conviction, could take part with gusto and a spirit of deep community friendship that went beyond any religious dogma and pomposity. Those who objected, and there weren't any, had the option of staying away.

By 6 pm, darkness fell. It was clear with a full moon. All had assembled in front of the Hall. There were three horse-drawn carts laden with food and drink including a barrel of the year's cider. In addition, there were two carts for the elderly and young children. Without exception all were dressed in seventeenth-century costume, some as Puritans and others as farmers, drummers, cavaliers and buxom serving wenches. Amrik who had dispensed with his turban, came with his team who had stripped the Hall of the armour from the walls. They came as pikemen and foot soldiers. Ash and the keepers were mounted dressed as Cromwell's Ironsides. The older children were carrying the guys they had made for the occasion.

Reverend Paddy appeared in full priest's uniform accompanied by his hound Gelert. The handheld beacons were lit. Paddy bellowed out a message in the style of an old version of the Book of Common Prayer:

"ACCEPT also, most gracious God, of our unfeigned thanks, for filling our hearts again with joy and gladness,

after the time that thou hast afflicted us, and putting a new song into our mouths, by bringing his Majesty King William upon this day, for the deliverance of our church and nation from Popish tyranny and arbitrary power. We adore the wisdom and justice of thy providence, which so timely interposed in our extreme danger, and disappointed all the designs of our enemies. We beseech thee, give us such a lively and lasting sense of what thou didst then, and hast since that time done for us, that we may not grow secure and careless in our obedience, by presuming upon thy great and undeserved goodness; but that it may lead us to repentance, and move us to be the more diligent and zealous in all the duties of our religion, which thou hast in a marvellous manner preserved to us. Let truth and justice, brotherly kindness and charity, devotion and piety, concord and unity, with all other virtues, so flourish among us, that they may be the stability of our times, and make this church a praise in the earth. All which we humbly beg for the sake of our blessed Lord and Saviour. Amen"

A massive cheer went up from the three hundred assembled. Torches were lit. The drums and bugles sounded, and the procession took off with Paddy at the front accompanied by Simon and Helen in simple Puritan dress. Many dogs attended with children holding them on leads.

Some twenty minutes later, they crossed the bridge over the stream and approached the castle. The area was lit with three beacons on poles.

All that remained was the keep and that was in good condition because subsequent earls had maintained it and it was kept locked. The only residents were a pair of peregrines that nested at the top. The castle had been built in the reign of

Henry II back in the twelfth century to dominate the locality The curtain walls and outer towers were largely gone with much of the materials used to build other housing, the church and some of the older barns.

The bonfire was on a flat space above the marsh about 200 yards from the castle. The foresters had used the wood taken from snedding the cut timber. It would be bright but would not burn for days.

From closer to the castle a cannon was fired, and this was a signal for the fire to be lit by the winner of the Guys competition chosen by the volume of the crowd's roar as each of the six Guys were presented. There was no surprise for the winner. This was a Guy in the form of the German Kaiser. Bitter memories remained of Queen Victoria's deranged grandson who was blamed for the deaths of millions whilst he remained alive and living in exiled luxury in a country that had profited from the convenience of neutrality in the conflict.

The huge bonfire blazed away. Amrik's team took over where tables were laid out with pies and sausages, tarts and relish. A pig had been roasting on a spit for the last four hours and was now ready to be carved by the keepers. The cider and other drinks were laid out. Simon and Helen dished out the drinks. Ash, Lisette, JJ and Julia helped out serving the food on thin wooden platters cut in the sawmill. The feasting went on for an hour, but the drinks continued as the crowd mixed and circulated. There was joy and laughter.

The cannon roared out again and sparklers were handed out to supervised children following which the cannon roared once more, the signal for Boynton to deal with the fireworks – some off which were home-made. All were totally spectacular, noisy in their effect and aimed over the marsh. None of the dogs seemed affected in the slightest but that was only to be expected on a shooting estate. At 10 pm the canon sounded again. Earl Simon thanked all those who attended for their hard work, comradeship and splendid company over the evening and invited those who wished to have another drink to do so as the embers slowly faded.

The evening went on but as the fireworks were now over folks gradually drifted away. Simon, Ash, JJ and their families remained till the end. The dogs feasted on the scraps from the pork. The castle looked stunning set against the full moon and the surface of the sea danced in the moonlight. With no other lights in the sky, the stars were on full display. Peace had returned. Simon produced a bottle of Jameson's and there was a bottle of ginger cordial for the children. They said little but enjoyed the moment for what it was. At midnight, they too, took the shortest routes back to their homes in the darkness.

The following Friday was another special day. The grey overcast clouds reflected the mood. The school half term was extended for the full week, so all were available to attend at the war memorial outside the church for the act of remembrance. Virtually the whole workforce and many from the village were present. All were smartly turned out as a mark of respect. Medals were worn. There were three Military Crosses and others wore their three campaign war medals of the Great War irreverently referred to as Pip, Squeak and Wilfred. There were medals from the Boer War and other campaigns, and some bore oak leaf motifs indicating a mention in despatches. Lisette wore her two medals. Boynton wore his Military Medal, the equal to the Military Cross but awarded to non-commissioned ranks. Many widows and their children attended wearing the medals of their late husbands on the right breast. All wore poppies.

And then there were the names on the memorial of those who had given their all. These were read out in turn. In most cases just the names and rarely a medal because gallantry medals are only awarded where gallantry was witnessed, but with so many there were no witnesses, or they too were lost in the same engagement.

Paddy presided. They sang 'Oh God our help in Ages past'.

One of the widows read from John 15:13 'Greater love hath no man than this, that a man lay down his life for his friends.'

A minute before 11 am, a bugle sounded with the last post. The union flag was lowered by a standard bearer.

Earl Simon spoke from Binyon's poem 'They shall grow not old as we that are left grow old. Age shall not weary them, nor the years condemn. At the going down of the sun and in the morning, we will remember them.' Those present echoed the words. "We will remember them".

Then, at the eleventh hour of the eleventh day of the eleventh month the church clock chimed eleven times, and two minutes silence followed. There was hardly a dry eye amongst the assembly. The sun emerged from behind a cloud and shone down bathing the memorial in light as the autumn leaves fluttered down in tribute. They sang the national anthem. Wreaths were laid. There was hope.

17

Royal rides and shots

November 1932

Joanna Johnson was eighteen years of age and nearing completion of her final Michaelmas term at the school that had moulded her over the past thirteen years. She was a fine violinist, academically bright and there was little doubt that she would move on to the Cambridge Veterinary School that she had selected. Horses had been her passion and close proximity to the estate's stables had facilitated this from her earliest memories. Over the past two years she had matured and blossomed into a raven-haired beauty, but unlike many others of her age, she had displayed no interest in the male attention that increasingly had come in her direction. All that was to suddenly change. On Sunday the twenty seventh of November at 10 am Jeremy de Lisle arrived at the Johnson household in his Austin 7, having been invited for lunch. Jeremy was coming up to his twenty first birthday. The rest of the family departed for church, but Joanna had been excused having been detailed to show Jeremy around the estate. Over the previous night, Joanna had been in a state of anxiety induced by a fear of the unknown at the prospect of what she saw as something of an imposed blind date.

On seeing Jeremy for the first time those fears were allayed. He was smart, dressed to ride but with a change of clothing for lunch, well-spoken and absolutely charming with a magnetic broad smile that disarmed and captivated. They shook hands and they looked into each other's eyes. The handshake lingered, as did their locking of eyes until both realised the length and gestured an apology.

They talked, in fact, they never stopped talking as they went to the stables, saddled up and took off around the estate for a two-hour ride through the woodland, along the beach and ending at the castle. It was readily apparent that they were totally on the same wavelength and shared the same interests and passions. Jeremy was unattached and was completing his final year at the veterinary school. It was a three-year course and after successful completion of examinations in June, he would be free to look for a placement.

At the castle tower they dismounted and walked around taking in the view over the salt marsh to the open sea. He reached out and took her hand. She took it willingly and as they walked the physical communication took over with gentle squeezes. They stopped, gazed at each other, then kissed.

"I'm sorry," said Jeremy. "Perhaps I shouldn't have done that. I've never had anything like this happen to me before."

"Me too," said Joanna. "But it was nice. It felt right." They kissed again and held each other not wanting the moment to end. Jeremy looked at his watch. It was 1230 pm.

"I suppose we had better get back. I don't want to upset your parents, well not on the first visit. First impressions are so important." said Jeremy.

"I agree," Joanna said. "My father being ex-military is a

stickler for punctuality, but you would know about that. That's something else we have in common. But you will come again, won't you?"

"Very much so. You may still be at school, but you are no schoolgirl. You are very much a grown woman and a woman I would very much like to share time with."

With that, they kissed and hugged again, then mounted up and cantered back to the stables.

Sunday lunch ensued. Jeremy was well received. Joanna was uncharacteristically forward and asked if Jeremy could return and stay for a few days after the end of term in two weeks' time. JJ agreed to that and said, "If that is what you would both like then we will be pleased to do that, but Joanna I just have one favour to ask. I would like you to take a day out of school next Wednesday. We have a very special shoot day coming up, and given your riding skills we have a very special job for you to perform. Can't say any more at this stage as things have to be confirmed but I'll come and get you on Tuesday at the end of the afternoon."

Joanna beamed with delight. "That's all right Papa. Wednesday is the least busy day with just sports after lunch."

Jeremy left at the end of the afternoon after a full expression of appreciation. Joanna walked him out to his car. Hands were squeezed and out of sight of the house, there was another kiss. Then, Jeremy started up the Austin and drove off into the sunset.

Wednesday the thirtieth of November was the most important day in the Spelthorpe shooting calendar. As was customary Simon as earl and estate owner would be invited as a guest to estates in Norfolk and neighbouring counties throughout the season and it was now his turn to host the annual visit. For this day there were two other earls, two viscounts, a baron and a duke. Simon would not be shooting himself as he had elected to load for the duke. As usual JJ would run the day, and Boynton would oversee the drives. Amrik and selected footmen were in their best attire to deal with the hospitality. Helen and Lisette would look after the ladies and Ash would oversee the picking-up.

On days such as this some of the invitees would bring their own dogs and have them on pegs whilst they shot. It was expected that they would have the opportunity to pick up if they wished so this needed careful management to ensure that they were not put out by other dogs running in unless it was for a wounded bird. Accordingly, Ash kept his other pickers up well back, and he managed the front with four of the merdogs. Hunter the diplomat and Odi the linguist had been assigned other duties.

In late November, darkness ruled, so there were just four shoot drives arranged for the day with three in the morning and just one for the afternoon close to the house. Boynton had anticipated this, and the first two drives would be along the eastern valley as the cover crops above the valley were bursting with game and had been left alone for the last two weeks.

An invitation had been sent to Sandringham for the king but as so often was the case, his diary was overloaded, and he was engaged launching new ships for the navy. Next in line was the Prince of Wales. He too, was out in the pursuit of leisure. He had inherited his grandfather's genes and was with a lady in the south of France. Accordingly, the invitation had gone down the list and had been gratefully accepted by the Duke of York, George V's second son. Simon was delighted at this. He was a keen shot and on previous days at Sandringham Simon got to know him as Bertie, his first name being Albert. Bertie loved the outdoors and Sandringham unlike his older brother who described it as 'too dull and boring for words' and considered it as a white elephant. Bertie always spoke with a bit of a stammer, but this was always much better when he was relaxed and with friends, although Simon took the view that his chain-smoking habit was not helping things. Bertie had been pleased to accept Simon's offer to load for him. He came with just his elder daughter Elizabeth. The duchess who had a heavy cold had elected to stay at Sandringham with their younger daughter. Three of the other guests had brought their ladies with them. Their chauffeurs would be loading for them.

The duke arrived in a Rolls Royce at 0915 with Elizabeth aged six who was dressed for riding. Bertie exited the Rolls and was greeted by Simon. The other guests were introduced, at the end of which Bertie said with a slight stammer. "Now listen everybody. Everybody calls me Bertie so no more of this Highness business. That's for formalities. We are all friends so it's Bertie from now on, and for the staff 'sir' will do nicely. I just want us all to make the most of a good day that I am sure Simon has arranged for us." He turned to Simon, "This is Elizabeth, and I know you have met her before, but in the family, we all call her Lillibet. I understand that you have a couple of lady riders who will be looking after her. But don't you worry. She will be fine. She's horse mad and has been riding since she was three." Simon introduced Joanna to Lillibet who took her hand. Together with Lisette, they took off to the stables accompanied by Hunter and Odi.

The shooting party took introductory drinks then headed off in the trailer for the first drive. They went to the far southern end on the eastern side where the valley was the deepest and the cover crops were on the hillside above. JJ positioned the guns along the valley bottom, and they waited for the opening two blasts of the whistle. Seconds later the sky was a mass of birds but driven in such a way that they didn't all come at once. Both Bertie and Simon were busily engaged for a full ten minutes. The duke shot well killing most in the air and many dropped at their feet because he took them early. On two occasions Simon had to guide Bertie to one side to avoid being hit by a tumbling weighty pheasant. Simon commented. "In the war we didn't get those Bodie steel helmets until the end of 1915, but with the way you are shooting Bertie, we will have to introduce a tweed version!"

Bertie confided in Simon, "I do so love coming here. That was spectacular. You are always so well organised on the drives and your keeper is a real magician at what he manages to pull off."

"He's a good man," said Simon. "With my deputy manager who runs the picking-up, they run the security side of this place. He misses nothing. His methods are what some would call unorthodox, but the bad boys stay away, and that's the way I like it. In the war he fought with that Lawrence of Arabia chappie, and he speaks fluent Arabic, not that there's a lot of call for that round here."

The duke responded. "It's a bit like the League of Nations round here, what with your keeper speaking Arabic, your manager and his wife fluent in French and to cap it all your good lady a Swahili speaker. And then you have your butler in the turban. This place brings back my childhood. My great-grandmother had her teacher, her munshi – Abdul Karin. I remember him at Windsor several times and at Sandringham when I was very young. He was such a kind fellow – always made a fuss of me. The queen adored him, and he doted on her. She showered him with honours, and that put a few noses out of joint. I think he was a Moslem, but he used to teach her Hindustani or something like that. Bit of a shame when my grandfather took over. He didn't like him and just threw him out. Burnt all his letters from the queen too. My father saw him in India on a visit a few years later. He liked him. Said he was very civil and humble. Most pleased to see him."

Simon added, "Our chap Amrik is a Sikh, so he speaks

Punjabi but is fluent in Swahili. He came over here with Helen from Kenya when we were married. She insisted on it. The man is totally loyal and hardworking and that is why we got him to run the household. The other staff respect him. That respect was earned. His wife runs the shop, and she is equally efficient. So, you are right, we are a bit unusual here. Even the border collie who is out with Lillibet understands both English and French what with Lisette spending half her life over there, but that's the British Empire. We seem to spend half our time all over the planet and we bring all the best bits back with us."

The duke concurred. "And long may that remain so, although I must confess, I still like the English countryside best of all and so do Elizabeth and the girls. That's why I'm quite glad that my brother David, that's Edward to those outside his friends and family, will end up as the next king and not me."

They carried on and did the next two drives which went as the first. After the second drive Amrik and his team arrived to serve sausages with mustard and sloe gin.

Bertie commented. "My God, these sausages are superb. Where did you get them?"

"These are our own recipe from our Tamworth pigs," said Simon." We have 200 at the moment but we will probably raise more because they are selling well. They spend a lot of time in the orchards and rooting out and wolfing down the acorns in the woods. That gives a fuller natural flavour. It's the Spelthorpe 'terroir' as the French would say. I'll get Amrik to put some in your Rolls for you to take back to Sandringham".

In the meantime, Lillibet had chosen the smaller of the Welsh mountain ponies as it was like her own at Sandringham. Lisette and Joanna took the cobs. Joanna kept very close and watched her every movement. For the first half mile down to the cottage they walked beside her. Lillibet was very confident. They decided that once they were beyond the dunes and over the soft sand, they would allow her to ride beside them. The dogs had made friends with Lillibet from the start but whilst they were riding, they walked behind watching all around. They saw a man in front of them. He was collecting driftwood. The dogs instinctively moved between him and the horses and although he waved, they both snarled and growled in his direction. They were, after all, on royal protection duty.

"Don't worry about that," said Lisette. "They do the same with me if I am alone and we see strangers. You are part of their pack now and they will look after you."

Lillibet responded. "My corgis are like that. We had a new gardener at home, and they bit him because he got too close, and they didn't know him."

Along the beach they went into a trot and then at Lillibet's insistence a short canter. When they approached the rocky area, they moved back to the edge of the woods. Lillibet asked, pointing to the pool. "Can I go and look over there? But I want to go on my own with just the dogs."

Lissette agreed. "You can go but you must stay in sight. We have to see you because your father would not be happy if we lost sight of you. Stay with the dogs. You can go for thirty minutes. We will wait here with the horses".

In an instant, she dismounted unaided and headed off a hundred yards away to the rocks. The dogs went slightly ahead. She followed them to the pool where the dogs sat down and waited for her to catch up. She cuddled both dogs on the edge of the pool. Suddenly there was a splash as Minerva surfaced.

"Hello, merdogs. I haven't seen you for a while. Who have you brought to see me?

"This is Lillibet. Her father is very important. He is a duke, and we are looking after her," said Hunter.

Minerva spoke to Lillibet and outlined what she had told the dogs back when they first met her. She explained that she was only visible to children under ten years old and animals. They had a conversation for a few minutes. Minerva promised the dogs that she would take them on another trip soon, then she turned and took off down the channel and back to the open sea.

Whilst they were with the horses, Joanna confided in Lisette about Jeremy's visit. Lisette had been a mentor to Joanna for several years and she would speak to Lisette about things she was thinking about but didn't want to tell her parents. She said, "I think I'm in love, but nothing has happened to me like that before. It's exciting and worrying at the same time. He's coming back to stay for a few days in a couple of weeks but the way I feel I want him to stay forever."

Lisette said. "These things can happen, and they happen at a pace of their own. It happened with Ash and I, but heart and head must be kept in balance. For us it was in wartime and there was a huge pressure to cast caution to the wind. We both had responsibilities, and we had to wait for a few months, but we got there, and you must do the same. If you have passions and things you can share that is good, but we are all individuals and have individual things we like to do, so private time is important too. If you can work together that helps, but the most important thing is total honesty with each other and talking things through. If you do that, if it is right, you will both come shining through."

"That helps me a lot. I needed to talk, and you are always so sensible, and you care and I appreciate that. Thank you so much." Joanna said to Lissette, and she squeezed her hand in appreciation.

Lillibet walked back to the horses.

"Did you have a good time?" asked Joanna.

"Yes, and I met a mermaid. She knows all about you and the

dogs. She calls them merdogs, and she takes them on exciting adventures," said Lillibet. "This ride with you has been wonderful and you are so kind to arrange for me to meet the mermaid."

Lisette explained to Joanna. "It's not as silly as it sounds" and she went on to tell her how both her and Ash had met up with Hunter and Odi at Étaples in the war and how Helen had met the mermaid with Kipling and Nimrod in Kenya. "I suppose you will think I'm as mad as the rest of them but that's my little secret and you must keep it like that as I keep yours." They all took the horses back at a walk to the stables, then went into the Hall and had lunch in a side room off from the main dining room.

The guests had a splendid lunch with fine wine that lasted a full two hours. Then at 3pm, they went off for the final drive of the day that Boynton had arranged to be quite close to the Hall as the light was fading.

Bertie had spoken to Lillibet prior to leaving for the last drive. She had gone back to the stables for an hour to see all the other horses. He confided in Simon again as he puffed away on another cigarette whilst they waited for the starting whistle.

"I really must thank you for this Simon. What you have done for me and how you conjured up that mermaid for Lillibet. That was absolutely amazing. I would like you to all come to Sandringham for a relaxed day, that's you and Helen of course, and your two managers with their families. It will be totally informal with a spot of shooting and and riding and can your man Ash bring those amazing dogs of his? I've never seen dogs work in such a coordinated way as that, and I want Elizabeth and young Margaret to meet them too."

Simon responded. "Well, that's exceptionally kind of you. We look forward to it."

The duke said. "Leave it to me I'll get my secretary to fix a date early in January when the Christmas fuss is over and before the children go back to school. I will make it a day when my brother is not there but that will be easy because he hates the place and straight after Boxing Day, he will be off with that appalling American woman. She's already got rid of husband number one. She's now on number two and she's carrying on with David. He's besotted with her, and I don't know why. She is so skinny and looks like a boy. Something very odd there. She is so rude. She openly refers to Elizabeth as 'Cookie' because she reminds her of an overweight Scottish cook from somewhere."

Simon added sympathetically. "Well, that's not very kind. It would be ungentlemanly of me to comment but I hope everything works out in time for you."

Bertie replied. "I hope so too. The king is tearing his hair out and I have this ominous feeling that the wheel is going to come off, but I hope not for everyone's sake.

The day went well with a total bag of nearly 600 birds, so all the guests were pleased. Good relations with the other estates would be assured. Most pleased of all was Boynton who they tipped generously and, as ever, he would share some of his tip money with the other two keepers.

18

Secrets of the keep

December 1932

Michaelmas term ended on Thursday the fifteenth of December. The pupils were excited to get away for the next three and a half weeks over the Christmas period, and Joanna who was especially looking forward to a three-day visit from Jeremy as of the following Monday. She was determined it would go well and made preparations to give her guest a memorable time.

The whole estate and village were preoccupied with Christmas decorations. There was a large, lit Christmas tree placed at the front of the Hall. The church had been decorated in a pagan style with wreaths and garlands of holly, ivy and yew in readiness for the carol service on the Sunday before Christmas. There were no big events planned other than carol singing on Christmas Eve around the large tree at the front of the Hall with a distribution of mulled wine and mince pies.

The dogs were pleased to see the return of Michael and Lucy. The morning swims had been abandoned although a traditional polar bear dip in the ocean was planned for the hardiest on

Boxing Day at noon. The dogs were happy enough to go on long walks of exploration around the estate. Victoria and Michael would continue to disappear on such walks, taking a pair of the merdogs with them on the basis that dogs tell no tales. All three children had asked to go picking-up on the final shoot on the Thursday before Christmas and whilst that was going on, Lisette, Helen and Julia had planned a last-minute shopping trip to Norwich.

All this activity presented few opportunities for the dogs to meet up with Minerva, but on the day the school broke up Trooper and Rafe managed to get away for a couple of hours. They dived in the pool with Minerva and surfaced in the same place but it was very different. The castle keep was still there but was surrounded by a wall with towers and a gatehouse. Men were still working on the walls. Where the brook entered the sea there was a jetty with fishing boats with sails and oars, but none were very large. Men were unloading herrings from the boat and women were packing some in barrels with salt, whilst others were being gutted and hung along poles that were placed in sheds from where there was a steady stream of smoke. The villagers were quite skinny and weathered in appearance and many had missing teeth. A few children appeared but they were all barefooted and poorly clothed. There was a small village of thatched low-level huts and houses. Smoke came out through gaps in the roofs. From the village and the castle was a foul-smelling ditch that poured into the brook. On the marsh were sheep, but they looked small in comparison to what the dogs knew. It was the same in respect of some long-horned cattle. The only creatures that looked the same were the red-brown hairy pigs that rummaged around the village.

Some soldiers appeared at the gate of the castle with a man they were guarding. He was naked but covered in long hair all over his body apart from the top of his head. The soldiers attempted to speak with the man. He just made grunting noises, but he remained compliant and the walked down to the sea to an area on the edge enclosed by three nets. The man swam in the sea and ducked under the water coming up outside of the nets but after a few minutes swam back and emerged. One of the soldiers gave him a fish from one of the boats, which he squeezed and then ate in its entirety.

The dogs were unsure and remained with Minerva. There were a few dogs in the village, but they seemed preoccupied with hunting out scraps and sitting by the tables where the fish were being prepared.

Trooper asked. "What is happening here Minerva?"

She responded. "I've taken you back over 750 years when the castle was first built. The hairy man was caught by fishermen in their nets about two months ago. They brought him back here. Bartholomew de Clanville, the knight in charge made him their prisoner in the castle dungeon. They tried to talk to him, but he just made grunting noises. They took him in the church but that made no difference. The people here were superstitious and thought anything from the sea other than fish was from the devil. They were frightened and didn't know what to do with him but if they killed him something bad might happen. The man has shown them no violence. They think he is a merman but as you can see, he has legs and no fishtail like me."

Rafe said, "What will happen to him then?"

Minerva continued. "In a few weeks' time when they bring him down to swim he will dive under the net and swim away, never to be seen again. But the story of the merman will remain and in many of the churches around here on the baptism fonts you will see carvings showing the merman or the wild man as some people called him. It's a good story and I don't know for sure, but I think the man is an unfortunate individual who has gone mad and not looked after himself. He probably stayed and didn't try to escape immediately because they sheltered and fed him."

Trooper said, "I'm not so happy here. There is something very odd about these people. They seem on edge. I much prefer living as we do now".

Minerva replied. "Those times were very different and very hard for ordinary people. They were violent times too. People were hungry, and if the harvest failed them, they would starve. There was always the threat of plague or illness, and in the civil war that took place 30 years earlier they said openly that Christ and the saints slept. People were very suspicious of anything they could not understand and blamed it on the devil. Most did not live beyond forty-five years of age and many died in childhood. I'll take you back."

They dived back into the pool and surfaced back in 1932.

Rafe said. "Thank you. It was interesting to go back so

far and see how things have changed. We are very busy at the moment but whenever we can get away, we will come and see you, even if we don't have the time to travel with you. We will tell the others."

With that, both dogs ran and splashed along the shoreline as they headed back to the cottage.

On the following Monday, Jeremy turned up at 9 am. Joanna rushed out on his arrival. They hugged briefly, and she took him inside. He presented Julia with chocolates and flowers and after settling into a guest room in the annexe, he emerged in riding gear. Downstairs Julia looked knowingly at her daughter. She could no longer treat her as she did a few months back. She simply said. "Be good Joanna and if you can't be good be careful!"

Joanna responded. "I know. Thank you, Mamma."

The pair took off towards the stables. In the stables, true feelings emerged. Joanna said. "I've missed you. Since last week all the time I have wanted you."

Jeremy expressed the same feeling, and they hugged before taking off down the track to the cottage and onto the beach where they galloped along the sands to the castle, where they dismounted.

They sat on a large log and looked over the sea. Jeremy talked about the role of the vet and how it was not just about treating sick or injured animals. He said. "A lot of what we do relates to the end of life for animals. They don't live as long as we do and quite often there is nothing we can do. Our professional code is about quality of life, and if that cannot be maintained then we must end that life as quickly and humanely as possible. The technical side of that is quite simple and I know on a lot of farms and here too that means using the wartime Webley. Farmers often say, 'Where you get livestock you get dead stock'.

Your hardest thing will be dealing with people who expect the impossible and try to equate animal longevity with human longevity but to prolong suffering is both cruel and selfish. I've seen this so many times working on placements and when I have been out with my father. I know that we only got together a short time ago, but things happen where a greater force steers us, and I felt that with you. I'm certain of that. I'm not trying to put you off, but I do not want you to be hurt because, Joanna, I love you and I can't put it any other way." With that he looked deep into her eyes and squeezed her hand firmly.

Joanna reached out and pulled him towards her. "I love you too. I can't explain why but they say that there is love at first sight and I felt that from the very beginning. What you have said is right and because you have said it in the way you did shows me how much you care. I have thought about what you said. I have seen this on the farm, but probably not as much as I need. I will make sure I get exposed and there are people here who will help me. A few weeks back I met our new policeman when I was out riding. He's been doing the job for about fifteen years. He lives in the village police house with his wife and two children. He told me that when he started, they deliberately made sure he went to all the horrible things, and they gave him all the death messages to deliver just to harden him up. He was fortunate because he has a farming background and had encountered quite a lot already,but many couldn't take it and there are a lot of people out there now who saw some horrible things in the war. Some came through unscathed and appear unaffected, but most have some mental scar tissue to a greater or lesser extent. Many just try to put it out of their minds and refuse to say anything about it but it's still there all bottled up inside ready to break out if something triggers it off".

They talked for about an hour, and it was clear to Jeremy that Joanna had a wisdom in advance of her years and that pleased him. They walked around the castle keep. Jeremy commented on the good state it was in.

Joanna explained. "My father makes sure the maintenance team look after it. They keep the wet out. It's so nice to have something like this. I know on a lot of estates they built pseudo castles and follies two centuries back, but we have a real one with a real history to it. They are jealous of what we have here.

A couple of the smaller rooms have been furnished with comfortable chairs and sofas and have fireplaces that we still use. There are benches and tables in the central hall, and we sometimes use it for family parties. You can go right to the top and outside, but we don't do that very often because we don't like to disturb the peregrines that nest up there. We are all right now because we are outside the breeding season and this year's two chicks have fledged. If you like we could come back here and have an early evening picnic dinner tomorrow I have the key. We can light a fire. It will be quite cosy with just the two of us".

"I'd like that very much," said Jeremy. "Are there any ghosts here?"

Joanna intimated that she had never met any in the past, but she told the story of the merman, though he couldn't haunt it because he didn't die there or anywhere nearby.

They mounted up and rode around the estate calling at the foresters' yard to visit the Suffolk Punch horses, then through the woods where the pigs were scoffing the acorns and the beech mast. Next it was on to the dairy. They rode past the church where Joanna pointed out the works opposite for the new veterinary surgery with the associated housing for the senior vet and any subsequent staff expansion. The works were well advanced.

Jeremy commented. "You haven't held back on this."

Joanna responded. "That's my father for you. Once a

decision has been made, he gets on with it, and it's an infectious habit that applies across the estate. It's that military discipline that endures with so many of the workers. As we own the land, we don't have a load of government officials slowing things up. I know he went to your father about the design and that was it. We have very good building team and the depression has helped. He got in touch with with some good local builders and tradesmen who were desperate for work, and they jumped at the opportunity."

"How do you know all this?" asked Jeremy.

"We always talk about these things over dinner at home and my papa is obviously aware of my career ambitions. I am also quite close to Lisette, Ash's wife. You haven't met them yet, but you will. She works part-time in the office and pays the bills. Ash manages the coastal and woodland section of the estate with the deer park, and he takes over the whole estate if my father is away for anything. It's a bit like the Roman Empire here with a triumvirate running the place but this one actually works, and they seem very close because they all served together in the war. Ash saved Earl Simon's life in a very nasty battle when many men from the estate were killed. He's also very good with dogs and runs the picking-up on the shoots. What do you think about the shooting Jeremy?"

"It's a difficult question," said Jeremy. "I've done it, but mainly pigeons and rabbits. There are so many people who just go to the butchers and buy their meat and haven't the faintest idea of what happens to get it there. Shooting and skill with arms is something that has always existed especially in the countryside and those skills have been useful to us as a nation. It's about survival. I don't have a problem if it is done quickly, cleanly, and the birds are eaten because then it's no different from a slaughterhouse, and at least the birds get a life beforehand so in that sense, on balance, I remain in favour. What I can't stand is when these spoilt city gents come out and think it's alright to blast at anything merely because they have loads of money. Half the time they can't even shoot straight because of the drink and the birds are pricked and maimed. That makes me angry. I know that doesn't happen here. It might sound extreme but if people are not prepared to kill, they shouldn't eat meat. I can respect the views of those who don't kill and are vegetarians but as a species we are omnivores and those who eat no meat or animal products can end up with deficiency diseases. The world we live in is getting very sanitised and that is not good. It's getting that some can live off the fat of the land and expect others to do all the dirty work but that's the endless debate between town and country. Self-reliance is essential for survival, but I'll get off my soap box and leave it at that."

They walked around the church and had a look inside. They saw the names on the memorial and counted them.

Jeremy commented. "There's a village in Kent, I think it's called Knowlton. They call it the bravest village in England because all the men volunteered, and ironically, they all survived. Should be the luckiest village in England compared to this place."

They went on to the estate shop where they met Jasmir (Amrik's wife) who showed them around and explained how she organised things. They bought a box of matches, two candles, and Jeremy selected a bottle of red wine for the return visit to the castle. As they left, Jeremy remarked. "What an absolutely delightful lady and so well organised. Is there anything they don't sell? That shop is such a splendid asset to the village and to have someone like that running it. I really like this place."

The light was getting low, so they returned to the stables. They met up with Jack one of the two grooms who looked after everything. He had been collecting dung from the paddock and was bedding the horses down for the night. He was of a similar age and gave them a short tour and explanation. They stabled the horses and walked back to the house in the twilight arm in arm.

On the following day after breakfast they walked down to the harbour and Jeremy was able to introduce himself. Then, after lunch they took a slow walk down to the cottage. Joanna had packed a bag of goodies, which Jeremy insisted on carrying. As they neared the cottage Nimrod and Kip bound out barking, but on recognising Joanna they stopped immediately, and their tails were wagging. All the dogs were present along with Michael, Lucy and Victoria who were engaged in an archery competition. Ash was out with Boynton, but Lisette was at home. Jeremy was introduced to Lisette. They chatted for about ten minutes then he went outside to meet up with the terrible three and all the dogs who were watching over them. Lisette told them that a sandwich and drink would be ready in half an hour.

When Jeremy was outside Lisette spoke quietly. It was the first opportunity since the royal visit.

"I can see what you mean, Joanna. You've got a good one there. I know I've only had a few minutes with him but that's female intuition for you. He's a keeper, and you make sure you fight to keep him. He will look after you. It was all in his body language towards you. That's the thing with men. They are quite simple to read but they wouldn't agree on that."

Joanna responded. "I'm glad you understand Lisette. The more time we spend together the more I realise that things are right for us. There will come a time when we will come out on that but it's early still, and, in the meantime, like you said we balance head and heart."

The gang came back into the house. Jeremy had been impressed by the demon archers. Jeremy and Joanna took coffee with Lisette who said. "We are the Spelthorpe hillbillies here and you have to treat us as you find us. We have no gas or running water, but that is going to change soon. We tend to spend rather a lot of time in the sea or the lake, but I'm sure all that cold water helps. We don't seem to get colds like so many others. What I wanted to say was that Boxing Day is the annual polar bear dip and those who have braved the ocean get a polar bear badge, or a bar to that if they have done it before. We have a bit of food and drink. Joanna's family will be coming and Earl Simon's, but I would like to see you too, if of course you are free. If you can't stay with Joanna, we can always fix you up here because it's no fun driving back in the dark."

"That would be splendid," said Jeremy. "I'm with my parents on Christmas Day like everybody else. My sister and her husband will be there. My father is renting a house at King's Lynn because it's easier to get elsewhere on military assignments, but he wants to be close to here so he can involve himself with the new surgery before he leaves the army in three months' time. It will be an absolute pleasure, and I will bring my swimming costume assuming that is required."

"Indeed, it is in mixed company," said Lisette. "Although it is suspected that us skinny dipper hillbillies don't bother on some occasions, but I'll say no more on that. I have heard that in Essex, they are setting up naturist camps but that is not something that Earl Simon would want us to follow up on at this stage, but you never know what is around the corner!"

After coffee the pair took off for the castle. There was a large padlock on the outside. They opened the door, and Joanna bolted it shut from the inside so they would not be disturbed. They went up to a small room on the first floor with a fireplace that led off from the main chamber. There was a sofa and an armchair. There were logs and kindling by the fireplace. Jeremy made up a fire which he lit. Joanna draped a sheet over the sofa. Whilst the fire got going, they went up and out on the roof because the light was failing. The view was impressive across the sea, along the pines and across to the Hall two miles in the distance, and they watched as the lights came on. Joanna placed her hands on the battlements and gazed out. Jeremy hugged her from behind and kissed the side of her neck. She felt him against her. She was happy. She was still passionate about the violin and the horses, but she had discovered something that she found she really wanted more than anything else.

They crept down the spiral stairs to the first floor. The flickering glow came from the anteroom. It was warm inside and Jeremy placed another log on the fire and lit the candles. There was a large sheepskin rug between the fire and the sofa. Jeremy placed the fire screen in front of the fire to keep any sparks at bay. They put the bag to one side and sat on the sofa locked together and talked, but discovered that they could enjoy the silence too. Jeremy wore just his shirt and moleskin trousers. Joanna wore a loose-fitting frock. They spent an hour in relaxation and togetherness.

Suddenly Joanna got up and spoke. "Wait here. I won't be a minute. I have something for you."

She went into the main hall to a chair and removed all her clothes. She walked slowly back into the room, leant down and kissed Jeremy from the back of the sofa. Then she walked around the front. Jeremy was taken aback. He said nothing but stared at the woman in front of him.

"My God," he said. "You are beautiful. Absolutely beautiful." Joanna beckoned him up. He rose and took her in his arms kissing her hungrily and passionately. She undid his shirt and as it fell to the ground she whispered in his ear, "Don't worry about anything. I finished yesterday so I'm safe."

"Are you sure?" he asked

"Yes absolutely, and I love you." With that, she undid his

belt. Then she took the sheet from the sofa and laid it on the sheepskin rug with two cushions underneath. She laid on the rug and then he got down beside her. They got closer and then gave themselves to one another.

An hour later they were still laying on the sheet over the rug. They made love again. It was longer then the first time but gentle and passionate. They dozed together for another hour and gazed into each other's eyes.

"This is what I want to do for the rest of my life," said Jeremy, "to wake up with you beside me. I know that it won't be every day, well not to start with, but that's what I want if you want that too".

"I want that so much. Meeting you has changed me forever. Is that a proposal?" she asked.

"Well, yes, it is. I can't really get down on one knee but yes, Joanna. Will you marry me?"

"Yes, yes, yes!" She kissed him again and again and again.

They lay together for a bit longer, then Joanna got up went out and returned a few minutes later.

She was fully clothed. Jeremy had dressed too. She said. "I know it's not very romantic but if you want a pee you will have to go outside. Our ancestors built splendid castles, but their sanitary provision was a little lacking."

He took the torch and wandered downstairs returning a few minutes later. Joanna picked up the single sheet. It bore the signs of a first-ever encounter so it went on the fire.

She opened the wine and the goodies she had prepared earlier. They ate and discussed the future, thinking how they would reveal their intentions. If things worked out Jeremy would come and live and work at Spelthorpe in July following his results. He explained that he had a placement at a surgery in King's Lynn coming up and this specifically related to surgery rather than pure medicine.

He said, "Diagnosis is about knowing the textbooks back to front and applying that knowledge having thoroughly analysed the signs, symptoms and history. Sometimes that might involve X-rays or exploratory operations and taking samples that only others might be able to look at. Sometimes a few pills or lotions might do the trick but, in my view, the real challenge is to go in and put things right surgically because that can make a huge difference. That is what I want to be able to do. Even after I qualify it might mean a week here or there working with a real expert to pick up from their knowledge and expertise by watching them and doing things under their supervision. That means a lot more than merely neutering cats and dogs. My father knows horses and farm stock inside out and I feel fairly confident with some of that, but if the business is to expand, we need to branch out a bit into small animals too. I'm sure you will get to Cambridge, which is a first-rate school. It is close enough to get back at weekends. I can always come and get you, and the train from Kings Lynn is quite good. You get quite long breaks between terms, and you will need placements. Most of those could be here. It will be a challenge, but together we will get there."

"You sound so positive," said Joanna, "and I like that".

"Have you done any lambing?" asked Jeremy.

"I've watched but that's it. Ash does a lot of that and runs things. He's very good, better than the shepherds, I would say because he is so well organised. He misses nothing. He runs the lambing sheds like a hospital ward, but he was a captain in the Royal Army Medical Corps in the war, so that's where it all comes from."

Jeremy continued. "Well at half term, go with Ash and get stuck in! It will stand you in good stead and for the veterinary school interview too – that's between seeing me, of course but we will find the time. I'll be there in the lambing sheds with you too and nothing beats a moment of passion rolling in the straw covered in sheep poo, milk and the bloody bits." He grinned. "I once emptied a bank like that a few years back when I was lambing and had to get some money. I walked into the bank with a sheepdog on a bit of string and I was covered in straw, muck and blood. Boy! did I get quick service! They wanted me out as soon as possible. But ultimately, it's one step at a time or one bite at a time if you want to eat an elephant. For the moment you must get the best grades in your school finals, and I will understand if there are times when you can't see me because of that but I will be there whenever you want me. Never forget that!"

Joanna just held him and kissed him again. "I love you so much," she said, "and I will work hard because it's for us now and not just me."

It was 9 pm, so they made sure the fire was safe and quietly left for the thirty -minute walk back to the annexe.

On the following day they rose at 7 am and breakfasted with the rest of the Johnson family. Jeremy behaved impeccably and was charming as ever. He intimated how impressed he had been with the way the estate was run and the speed at which works were undertaken. Joanna explained that they were going to explore the south side before Jeremy had to return home and that they had met up with Lisette who had invited Jeremy to join them on the Boxing Day polar bear dip.

Julian said. "That's excellent. Then we will find out what you are really made of when you swim amidst the Norfolk icebergs. You must stay the night here afterwards. They are quite remarkable, the Cromwell team, the way they swim virtually all year round, but I suppose it saves on bath water. I just wonder if they will go soft when we plumb them in with gas and running water. They don't seem overly excited about that because they enjoy living in the Stone Age with that pack of dogs. Secretly I'm quite jealous because they are all as tough as can be and Victoria, the earl's daughter, has taken to it because she seems to spend most of her time down there. Those dogs are remarkable, so much so that after Christmas, we are all off to Sandringham for the day for a spot of shooting and curiously so the duchess and Margaret Rose – the younger daughter, can meet up with them. The duke was really impressed when he was here three weeks ago. He is such a nice chap, modest and quiet but he really adores living up this way – like chalk and cheese, him and his brother. Joanna looked after the elder daughter, and she was very impressed. I was wondering Joanna, we haven't had much from you on the violin recently. I would very much like it if you and Jennifer could do something for them when we go up there. Jennifer is still in bed, but it's a holiday and she needs her growth sleep. She is superb on the piano too, so I was thinking a bit of 'The Lark Ascending'. That should impress the duke. I can't think of anything better – so serene. It's England captivated in eleven minutes, and you will probably think I 'm an old softie for a military man but I have to admit it brings a tear to my eye whenever I hear it. Joanna does it brilliantly. Anyway, I've got to dash now. Nice to have you here. There's just one thing, but keep it under wraps. I've spoken to the earl and when you qualify which I gather from your father is a cert on your past performance there will be a job here for you too. I'll see you on Boxing Day."

And with that he was off.

Jeremy and Joanna sat with Julia for a while then Jeremy went upstairs to change. Julia spoke to her daughter. There were tears in her eyes. "Don't think that we have not noticed the transformation in you. You are like a butterfly that has suddenly emerged from its chrysalis. You are no longer a schoolgirl, and we can see that feelings are deep, but we want you to always be our daughter. We are both proud of what you have achieved but we recognise that things are different now and you have to make your own way. We both love you so we will work out a way ahead, but you should know that we both like Jeremy, and we know he will look after you and you him. It's just been a bit of a shock, but we know these things happen quickly but never forget that we are there for you."

Joanna responded. "Thank you for saying that Mamma. There is a lot to think about, but it is 'we' now and not just me anymore and neither of us wants to let you down. We just need a bit of time, and we are talking a lot."

The pair left the home shortly afterwards. This time they selected two of the fine Suffolk Punch horses for a change and took off down the main drive and across the road and railway line onto the southern section of the estate. They went into the residential part where many of the workers lived and encountered Rev Paddy Collins on his rounds. He had his best friend, the mighty, gentle Gelert with him. They dismounted and Joanna introduced Jeremy. Paddy mentioned the new building opposite the church and the speed at which it was going up "Remember this from the letter to the Hebrews '*Every house is builded by some man; but he that built all things is God*' and I'm sure that God wants to see you both there so when are you two going to be getting married?"

Jeremy responded "Well that's not something we have announced. Who told you that?"

"Well," said Paddy. "As soon as I saw you together, I saw not two people but one. That's what the Lord directed me to say, and you haven't denied it, so now I that it's true so, I'll be seeing you both in the church before the end of summer. I know that to be sure."

Joanna came into the conversation. "Thank you for your blessing but you are the only one who knows, Paddy. Can we ask that that stays with you until we come back to you as we most certainly will."

"Indeed, that will be," said Paddy. "So I bless you both and the Lord will go with you. Now, I have visits to make and I'll be seeing you, and a happy Christmas."

Paddy walked on.

"He's very perceptive," commented Jeremy.

"Yes, and you won't find a finer vicar anywhere. He spent time in the trenches in France and the soldiers had nothing but good to say of him. There's no pomposity with him and his sermons are short and straight to the point. We are so lucky to have him," said Joanna.

The pair mounted up and rode on. The horses were pleased with the outing as normally they were just on cart or plough work. They talked to them reassuringly as they rode, and it was evident the change of scenery was welcome to them. They rode through the deer park, up to the southern gate and down the length of the wooded valley that took them back to the castle.

"That will be our place, our special place," said Joanna.

"It was a beautiful thing and a beautiful way to start our lives together," said Jeremy. "And whilst it might be tempting to go back, to do that too early would cheapen what we experienced, and I would never want to do that. I want to make love to you again so much and I will miss you until Boxing Day but after that I will arrange for you to come and see my parents. There will be something special after that in the time before you go off to Sandringham."

They rode back along the sand and onwards to stable the horses. They returned to the annexe somewhat more relaxed following

Joanna's conversation with her mother, which had indicated that open signs of mutual affection would not be frowned upon. As daylight dimmed, Jeremy set out for the one-hour return to King's Lynn.

19

Polar bears and 'The Lark Ascending'

Christmas had followed the usual pattern at Spelthorpe: carols on Christmas Eve, a short church service on Christmas Day followed by the usual family meal. Simon, Ash and JJ had been up before first light to take care of any livestock issues and to milk the dairy herd to afford the workers with young children a spot of Christmas magic.

Simon and JJ had Christmas dinner at the Hall as neither had extended families. Presents were handed out before dinner. Victoria was delighted with her longbow. Amrik and the live-in domestic staff took their Christmas dinner later in the day with Simon, JJ and the ladies serving in role reversal. This only happened on two days in the year, but the exercise in humility paid dividends in loyalty. Ash and Lisette dined in the cottage on a rib of beef. Ash's parents spent the day with them and the twins.

Jeremy de Lisle turned up at the annexe at Spelthorpe Hall at 9 am on Boxing Day. He brought presents: a Swiss Army knife for

Julian and miniatures of Parfum Chanel No 5 eau de parfum for the ladies. Joanna took him up to the large guest room at the end of the upstairs corridor. It looked out over the lake with a Juliette balcony and French doors and had a small ante room with washing and toilet facilities. There was a double bed.

" My mother insisted you be upgraded to this," she said. "I think she likes you." They went downstairs and had coffee with Julian and Julia. Jennifer had gone out for an early morning ride, taking Zulu from the Hall along as an escort.

After pleasantries had been exchanged in which Julian instructed that both he and Julia would be addressed by Christian names henceforth then Julian came straight out with it:

"I understand that you two want to get married."

Both Jeremy and Joanna were somewhat taken aback by the suddenness of the declaration. After a brief silence Jeremy responded. "Yes, that's absolutely right. We both love each other and in the three days I spent here, we came up with a plan, but we didn't want to disclose matters too soon lest we incur your wrath. We had aimed at keeping things low-key until Joanna finishes school because nothing must compromise her getting the best possible grades and I need to come through my studies with flying colours but at the same time we need to be with each other as much as those major considerations allow. Is that a fair summary, Joanna?"

"That's right," said Joanna. "I've spoken to Mamma, and she knows how deeply we feel for each other. It's heart and head and getting the balance right, but I love Jeremy and whatever happens we will marry, and you know how determined I am, but we want to do it right."

Julian was silent and reflected. Then he said. "We worked out what you would say so here is our decision. We know it would make no sense to try to stop things. That would be as stupid as trying to stop the tide coming in. Your mother and

I had similar experiences and emotions at your age, and we do not want to lose either of you. You both have our support because your prospects are sound, both of you, and I know that's always what fathers come out with on these occasions. As far as we are concerned, from this moment within this household and with the knowledge of two others and their wives who we trust implicitly you are both engaged to be married. That does not extend to their chatterbox children. There will be no hint or mention of this in or in connection with the school. An announcement will come on the day after you leave the school for good. We know that your marital status does not apply to further education.

If you have or are going to buy a ring that will only be worn away from here. We have allocated the end guest room for both of you and we trust that you will exercise good sense in that respect. Jeremy is welcome here at any time. Now that may sound like we are being over liberal, but as you know I can't stand those bloody Liberals. I try to be thoroughly realistic and pragmatic about everything and to get things done without needless undue fuss. After much thought that is the way we will keep you, and there will be no need for secrecy or dishonesty as to where you are at any time. We want you to be safe. So, is that understood and agreed? I will expect you both to enlighten your father and mother, Jeremy."

Joanna answered. "That is so kind of you. We thank you. That is more than we expected, and we will keep that trust. I love you both."

Julian went outside. Jennifer had returned and they were speaking outside for a while.

He came back with Jennifer and a bottle of Champagne which he opened and poured into five glasses. "Here's to you both. We wish you health and happiness, and as it's Christmas in the words of Tiny Tim: God bless us everyone!"

Joanna couldn't help relating the conversation they had had with Paddy just before Christmas. Julia said." We know Paddy. He's an absolute darling. He looks like God and half the people round here think he is God, so our secret will be safe with him".

They all got ready with swimming costumes under their clothing and took off for the cottage on foot bearing gifts. Not gold, frankincense and myrrh, but something to be consumed on the spot. Lisette welcomed them all and instructed them on the changing facilities: Ladies inside; gents in the barn and with the merdogs, Zulu and Siamese cats anywhere they wanted to be. They assembled and walked through the gap. Fortunately, the tide was fully in.

Ash and Simon sidled up to Joanna and Jeremy and whispered. "Congratulations to you both. Glad to have you on board." Helen and Lisette did the same. Towels and dressing gowns were placed on the edge of the dunes. For Edward and George, it was their initiation to this Spartan activity. They all lined up, all fourteen of them plus the dogs. The sea was calm. There was a chill in the air but no wind. On the stroke of midday, Ash drew his Webley revolver loaded with blanks and fired into the air and they charged. There would be no retreat on this day for the glorious charge of the Spelthorpe Brigade. The cries of 'Charge' resounded in the air. They hit the sea running and flung themselves forward and submerged. Then they did an about-turn leaving behind Ash, Lisette, Michael, Lucy and the merdogs to stay a little longer along with Jeremy and Joanna who were ecstatic with the earlier revelation. They were determined to mark the occasion by remaining a while longer. The merdogs were showing off, duck-diving and coming up half a minute later. After five minutes, they all got out. Ash and Lisette's hardy pack could have remained, but she was conscious of her duties as a hostess.

Contrary to expectations, they were all walking on the sand still unwrapped as the shock had produced a reaction where all the warmth had gone to the centre of their bodies and they felt a tingling, glowing invincibility despite the chill in the air. Lisette declared. "Now you've all had a wash, I can let you back into my house." After savouring the moment and taking in the view of the pines along towards the castle they headed back to the cottage. The merdogs remained on the edge and appeared to be engaged with somebody unseen.

Lisette, Helen and Joanna realised that it must have been the mermaid, although they never saw for themselves. A few minutes later the merdogs came back to the house with tails wagging.

Lisette had prepared well with a tureen of French onion soup with croutons and cheese. There were plenty of the Spelthorpe sausages with jacket potatoes and a large bowl of warmed mulled wine – all intended to warm the assembled company. At mid-afternoon there was a presentation of embroidered polar bear badges and bars marked with the year.

Joanna sat with Jeremy as he befriended the merdogs. They were keen to introduce themselves to the new family member. She had taken Jeremy into her confidence regarding the intriguing events of the last four months. He had noted their duck-diving for himself, and as the dogs offered front paws in friendship, he could not help but notice the extended webbing between the dogs' toes. It was clearly unusual for dogs, particularly as all came from different litters and some from elsewhere than Norfolk. It was certainly a superb tale, but he concurred that there are times when it was best to let sleeping dogs lie. Any scientific investigation would only serve to spoil the magic. Later, they both had a chance to talk with Ash. They had much to thank him for as they had heard that it was he who had raised the veterinary needs of the estate and without that they would have never come together. Jeremy raised the issue of 'hands-on experience' for Joanna, and he agreed to take her under his wing for the lambing that would take off in February. The twins picked up on the fact that Joanna had got a boyfriend. Joanna played it down by simply saying to Michael. "And you have had a girlfriend for months!" He said no more.

With all the activity over the last two days, tiredness had started to set in, so sincere thanks were expressed. Simon and Julian's families took their leave at 6 pm. Both Joanna and Jeremy were worn out by the nervous energy of recent development, so after a night cap, they retired. Jeremy and Joanna went upstairs. Jeremy went to the large guest room. Joanna whispered. "I'll be along shortly."

On a visit to King's Lynn three days earlier, Jeremy had prepared himself. The chemist was always potentially embarrassing if a lady was serving or if the shop was crowded, and one of his friends had confessed to going in several times only to emerge with aspirin on each occasion. Jeremy had opted for a haircut instead, on completion of which the barber asked, "Anything for the weekend, sir?"

"Yes please," said Jeremy. "I'll take a dozen." The goods were handed over.

"No point in wishing you a good weekend," said the barber. "It looks like you have got it sorted. I'm envious!"

Jeremy was in bed wearing just pyjama bottoms. The lights were out, and he dozed. He had left a couple of the packets in the bedside cabinet drawer so any prying eyes would be reassured, not that he suspected that it might happen.

A few minutes later he felt a warmth next to him and passions were raised.

They woke to the dawn in each other's arms and gazed at

each other. It was the best feeling in the world, and they didn't want it to end. They felt happy and fulfilled.

At breakfast the whole family were present. Joanna was visibly glowing as her newfound joy reflected in her demeanour. Jeremy said that he and Joanna would be going to see his parents the following day, but they would be back by the weekend. They planned a further ride of exploration for the day and Jeremy asked Jennifer to come along with them. She beamed at the offer of inclusion and accepted gladly. Julian reminded his daughters that a royal performance was coming up. A rehearsal would be prudent, and it was agreed that part of the afternoon would be allocated for this. They took off mid-morning and selected three of the Suffolk Punch horses. They didn't get the same attention as the ponies, so it was important to keep them in the team. They all recognised that deep down horses are sensitive, affectionate creatures who respond to any special attention.

They called at the cottage. Michael and Victoria were testing her new bow. Lucy had gone out for the day with her father in the truck along with Trooper and Rafe. Joanna had a moment with her mentor. She thanked Lisette for her support.

They rode on to the castle with Nimrod and Kipling in tow. Although they were Ash's dogs, they were seen as estate dogs and with permission would latch on to the greater family. They rode down onto the marsh where the Romney Marsh sheep were grazing. Their rumps still bore the tell-tale coloured patches indicating which ram had serviced them. The lambs would arrive at Easter. They dismounted and walked over to where the dozen Highland cattle were grazing. These ginger, shaggy, affectionate beasts craved human attention. They dealt with the tougher grasses and vegetation and provided an atmospheric, ornamental addition to the castle, so rearing for meat was not a priority. Any surplus numbers were usually sold on to other estates.

They rode on and met up with Amos the shepherd and later encountered Boynton who was setting out to feed his pheasants. He had a roll up cigarette dangling from his lip. As ladies were present Boynton was a model of charm. He invited them into the cottage and offered them a Christmas shot of Jameson's. Jennifer was a little hesitant about that, but Boynton said, "Don't worry lass. I won't tell your mum. It will help maintain your radiant beauty." Whilst the girls were petting Black and Tan, Boynton went outside with Jeremy. He returned to his normal vernacular with a few choice words in his conversation. "I hear your father is coming here as the vet. That's long overdue. Just what we need. Will you be joining him?" Jeremy explained that he expected to qualify in the summer and wanted to join the team. "Well you'll be coming to the right place. His lordship, Ash – that's my boss and Mr Johnson are good blokes. Good to me but if you want help with anything I'll sort you out. I know this place like the back of my hand so if you're stuck come and see Boynton. That's what they all call me, but never use my first name. I hate it." With that they shook hands firmly as the girls emerged from the cottage with all four dogs around them.

They remounted and went on. Julia commented. "Now you've met Boynton. He's a good man, keeps us all safe and Papa always says he's glad Boynton is on our side. We don't get any poachers around here. They are all terrified of him. He's a brilliant keeper."

They rode back to the cottage where they parted with the dogs and continued back to the stables.

In the afternoon, the rehearsal went well. Jeremy went for a walk down to the churchyard and returned in time for the final performance. He was moved by what he heard, not having experienced it before. He said to Joanna afterwards, "Not only have I won the most beautiful woman in Norfolk but someone who can take an audience to heaven and back, and your sister is brilliant too!"

On the following day they took off quite early for the trip to Jeremy's parents who had rented a modest cottage on the outskirts of Kings' Lynn. Both greeted the news of the arrangement with enthusiasm. Rufus went into the garden with his son. "I always knew you were an achiever but how you pulled this off is amazing. I met Joanna when I was down there with her father, but you have left me speechless. She is a genuinely lovely girl although I should say woman. I can't wait to get started down there. You tell me it's all coming on at a pace so I'll be down periodically to make sure we can hit the ground running. The army was good, but the time is right to move on to a new challenge and I'm sure that we will pull it off. All you have got to do now is to get through that course. I know you will crack it, but leave nothing to chance, and you know, we are there for both of you."

The couple stayed for an early lunch. Jeremy collected some books, clothing and things and said they were going down to Cambridge to show her the veterinary school, and they would then be working their way back to Spelthorpe.

By 1 pm they were on their way. Jeremy made a brief stop in Ely on the way to Cambridge and asked Joanna to wait in the car. When he returned, they continued their journey. "What was that about?" asked Joanna.

"Don't worry," he said. "Just something I had to sort out. You will find out later. You must let me give you a few surprises."

In Cambridge the first place they visited was a jeweller's shop. The staff recognised Jeremy and produced an engagement ring "Well, what do you think?" he asked. "Try it on."

Joanna tried the ring. "It's beautiful. I love it and it fits perfectly."

"You're not just saying that," asked Jeremy.

"No, I mean it. It makes me feel like a real princess, but it's bound to be too expensive."

"Then you shall have it then," replied Jeremy. "If we are spending the rest of our lives together then only the best will do and don't worry about the money. I've worked a lot helping out at veterinary practices in the holidays and saved a lot and my grandmother left me a tidy sum when she passed, so we have no worries in that direction."

"How did you know it would fit?" she asked.

"I would have thought that was obvious. On the day after the castle when I was playing with your fingers and a bit of tape, I measured your finger and marked the tape with a fold." he replied.

"You're a cunning one," she said.

"No, just well prepared. It's always about thinking ahead and leaving nothing to chance." He replied.

"Well, there's no doubt there; you're just like Papa. You will fit in well at Spelthorpe."

Jeremy handed over some cash and pocketed the sapphire and diamond ring.

"You will get that tomorrow," he said. "We are going somewhere special for that."

They went on to the veterinary school. Jeremy called on the bursar and he introduced Joanna as a friend who wanted to study there. Then he went to his room and collected some notes and books and gave Joanna a lightning tour. He told her that at Easter, he would bring her back when they would have a couple of days in Cambridge.

After that, they drove back to Ely. There was no mistaking the place with its magnificent cathedral that dominated the fenland, but it was totally disproportionate in size to a city that was little more than a large village. When the Normans conquered England, Ely had been one of the centres of resistance and rebellion under Hereward the Wake. Hereward got away and disappeared following a siege, but the Normans wanted to stamp their mark and authority over the land. They did that by building castles and God's castles in the form of cathedrals as a way of making atonement for all the slaughter and spilling of Christian blood which was something they were not supposed to do. Cathedrals provided a pragmatic solution. The Normans did the killing, and the monks installed at cathedrals and Norman abbeys across the land did all the praying that was needed to balance the heavenly books.

They parked up in the city and went to an old hotel that was a stone's throw from the cathedral. He dipped into his pocket and produced a simple wedding band. It looked like gold, but it was mainly brass.

"What's this for?" she asked.

"You are now Mrs. Jeremy de Lisle of Church View Cottage, Spelthorpe! I know our future home is not fully built yet, but some of these old hotels want both guests to sign the register and the snotty owners think Victoria is still on the throne so slip this on your finger and we will be alright. The jeweller threw this in for nothing, and I should think so."

She kissed him. "You are amazing. You think of everything, and I love you."

They entered the hotel and passed the morality checks with flying colours. They went up to the room. It had a four-poster bed with a mattress you could sink into and disappear. There was an exposed beam ceiling and leaded windows, and it was almost like the next stage up from the castle.

"I know I plotted the castle, but you are a romantic devil. I love this," said Joanna.

They dined at the hotel and woke up together for the third night in a row.

After breakfast they took a walk to the cathedral. Neither had been inside before. It had been decorated for the festive season but there were few people about. It was impressive particularly the massive octagonal tower and lantern. They walked around looking at the carvings, the stained glass and memorials. At the far end of the choir aisle, they came across a small chapel. There was an inscription in Latin above the arched door which Jeremy translated as 'By the grace of God I am what I am'. He continued. "I suppose that's why we are here, because we are what we are and although I'm no fanatic of religion I have always felt that there was a greater hand that steers our destiny."

"You know Latin then." said Joanna.

"Yes, I did five years of it at Wellington College. It's a school with a strong military connection and that's why my father sent me there. It happens so often with officers' sons with them being posted all over the place. They lost over 700 former pupils in the war – all volunteers, all those talented lives wasted. Most were mere subalterns and young officers in the trenches saying to their men, 'Follow me chaps' as they went over the top. And that's not a record. For Eton it was about 1,100 – a far worse tally when matched against mainstream volunteers who enlisted. As they say one death is a tragedy. More than that is a statistic. Sorry if I sound morbid but that's the military for you. They are a family, and I've noticed those strong bonds at Spelthorpe. Anyway, I found the Latin quite handy on the medicine side of my studies. Have you done it?" he asked.

"I did it for five years too and passed the standard examination so I'm sure that will come back to me. For the last two years it's been mainly biology and chemistry for me, along with history and French but that was a choice to match what I intended doing and without the first two, a veterinary career would have been impossible".

They went into the chapel and sat side by side. "I thought

somewhere like this would be the best place to put that ring on your finger. I'll make a silent prayer for us both," said Jeremy.

"And I will do the same," said Joanna. "It's just a shame that when we get back to Spelthorpe I will have to take it off and keep it safe but that is the agreement, and we will stick to that but I will show Mamma, Lisette and Helen first before I do that. I'll wear my gloves when we get back." Jeremy took out the ring and placed it on her finger whist they maintained a long eye contact. Then they held each other in silence for a few minutes before they walked on.

They walked back to the hotel and passed the house where Oliver Cromwell lived for many years. It was only 11am. They decided to check out rather than stay another night having fulfilled the purpose of the trip, so they took a slow drive back to Spelthorpe, getting home just after 2 pm.

Joanna was excited and couldn't wait to show off the ring. Joanna insisted that Jeremy go with her. The Johnsons were out so they set of on foot, first to the Hall where they saw Helen who beamed when the glove was removed. A similar reaction took place at the cottage then they went back to the annexe where her mother had returned. The quality of the ring and stones confirmed that Jeremy was absolutely serious and robust in his intentions and would accept nothing but the best for her daughter and he was not one to put things off. That was reassuring to her and for the first time she gave Jeremy a huge hug. Joanna took off the ring and put it back in the box and said to her mother. "And that's where it will be staying until my last day at school. We both have work to do and we will help each other with that. Having a goal has made a huge difference to both of us."

Jeremy stayed at the annexe with Joanna for the rest of the holiday. They both set aside two hours every day for revision and study but there was always time in every day to ride the horses along the pines and seashore and to demonstrate their affection in private.

Wednesday 4th January arrived, the set day for the visit to Sandringham. Jeremy undertook to look after Zulu for the day. Three black cars assembled at the front of the house and as the three men loaded the cars with gun, and the violin and cello cases, it looked reminiscent of an American gangster movie. The merdogs and children were distributed as they best fitted in, and Simon made sure that the tray of Spelthorpe sausages were placed well out the way of any voracious Labrador.

The drive to Sandringham took just over the hour. They were admitted through the wrought iron gates and drove the half mile up to the front of the house. The duke with Elizabeth and the girls were at the front door to welcome them signalling a departure from the usual protocols and indicating this was a visit from friends. The duke was beaming and indicated that all adults were to be on Christian name terms for the duration. Lillibet bounded out with her younger sister crying out. "It's the merdogs!" And she ran into the midst of them. They reciprocated her affection. She spotted Joanna and ran across and hugged her saying. "You must come up to the stable to see my horses!"

After drinks, Bertie indicated the arrangements for the day. "We have three drives this morning. Elizabeth wants to see your fantastic dogs in action so she will come with Margaret Rose who is impervious to gunfire. She loves the bangs! We will all load for ourselves and from what I have seen your dogs will do all the picking-up required. I just have one keeper who will load the birds on the truck and that will be it. My head keeper will run things, and he has two underkeepers who will run the beaters. I have arranged for one of the grooms to take Lillibet and Joanna up to the stable, and the ladies may watch the shoot or go to the stables. We aim to finish that for lunch just after midday and I had a call that you are going to give us a musical performance. We have a nice piano in our large sitting room so that should be ideal."

They set off as directed. With just half the usual number of guns, it was easy to organise and at Ash's command, the dogs set themselves out forty yards behind the guns with Michael and Lucy there for direction if needed. They were used to working with the pack. Elizabeth was intrigued to see the border collie in the line.

"You just watch her!" said Ash. "That will be a first for Sandringham".

The shooting went well. It was expertly managed, but the birds were no match for three decorated war veterans from a shooting estate who apart from Simon specialised in wood pigeons. Hardly anything got through. Bertie shot well on his own ground. As ever the dogs worked as a team covering each other with Trooper and Rafe directing and dropping the game by the gun cart. Elizabeth was amazed at how they did it without all the waving and shouting to which she was accustomed and when she saw Odi darting in and out at lightning speed, she stood with her mouth open in amazement.

Lunch was taken in the smaller dining room. For the main course they had liver pâté followed by lobster. Joanna and Jennifer ate with the adults whilst the younger children were taken off for lunch and games with members of the household staff. Ash explained his training methods to the duchess who was intrigued. "The dogs want to please and they have senses that are far more acute than ours so it's merely a case of capitalising on that and getting the more experienced dogs to train the youngsters. Tying a dog to a peg merely frustrates the dog and is symptomatic of somebody who doesn't want to put the time in. At the end they just play at it and send their dogs to pick up birds a few feet away that they could pick up themselves. Might as well go round with a vacuum cleaner! I know that some might find that shocking and insist on convention, but you did ask me, and my priority is always to get wounded birds and deal with them as quickly and humanely as possible." Elizabeth said, "I think that is a very kind way of doing it and I know how distressed some of my friends have been on seeing wounded birds. On reflection you are absolutely right. Lillibet keeps talking to me about the merdogs and this mysterious mermaid. Can you enlighten me".

Ash responded. "I think Helen and Lisette can explain all that to you. It's an incredible tale and we will tell it to you as valued friends on the basis that it stays in the room. You might think at the end that we should all be committed to the local lunatic asylum. Fortunately, it is all deniable because the last thing we want is the press all over the place."

"Absolutely!" said Bertie. "Those people can be a bloody nuisance at times and what is private stays private, so you have our total assurance on that."

And so, Helen and Lisette related the tale of the merdogs or at least what they knew of it, including the fact that it had been noticed that the dogs displayed a mutation of the front paws.

Bertie came in at the end. "That's a remarkable story and I won't dismiss it because Lillibet always tells the truth. She's passionate about what she likes, but deep down, she's serious and there are things out there, uncanny things that we can't work out. We know things now that 200 years back they would have been aghast at, like flying for example, and now that Mitchell man is making sea planes that fly at 400 miles an hour. Who would have believed that in 1733? But have no fears your secret is safe with us! I don't want those press men saying I've inherited something from my Great- Great -Grandfather George. He used to have long conversations with oak trees at Windsor apparently".

Simon then came in with the developments at Spelthorpe and mentioned the runways and the Gipsy Moth plane that he had ordered. He invited Bertie to come over as soon as they were up and running. He also outlined the plans for new veterinary surgery with Major Rufus de Lisle who would be setting things up in the months ahead. Bertie seemed interested in that as he knew that really good horse vets were in short supply. The military had the best and he hinted that he might end up as a client.

It was then that the conversation turned to the duke's brother and his relationship with Mrs Simpson. There were things that were probably best left unsaid, but it became obvious that Elizabeth loathed the woman. The Spelthorpe Company listened sympathetically but made no comment.

The duke proposed that they retire to the large sitting room for coffees and brandy. That was a signal for the Johnson girls to ready themselves for their performance and sensibly they had stayed off the alcohol. They had packed elegant black dresses which they changed into, so they looked totally professional. The performance started with Elgar's 'Cello Concerto', with Jennifer taking the lead and Joanna in support on the violin. This was followed by Joanna on the violin with Jennifer supporting on the piano for Vaughan Williams' 'The Lark Ascending'. With just two instruments any musical work normally played with orchestral accompaniment would mean limitations, but the girls had prepared for that and made slight adaptions. Their passion and technical ability produced a performance that was transcendent. Julian and Julia beamed with pride at their daughters' achievement.

There was total silence at the end. The audience was spellbound. Bertie was moved to tears. He stood up and Elizabeth joined him. They clapped and clapped and clapped.

"That was sublime." Bertie said. "I've been to performances before but nothing with such subtlety and passion". He walked over to the girls. He gently shook their hands and gave each a little kiss as a demonstration of his heartfelt appreciation.

As the day came to an end, expressions of gratitude were exchanged. It was apparent that Bertie and Elizabeth had found friends whom they would treat as genuine with the intimacy that entailed. The duke gave Simon a special phone number that would bypass the usual filtration to get directly to him and Elizabeth. Mutual assurances were made of further visits. Lillibet was thrilled that she would get to see Lisette, Joanna and the merdogs in the future.

In the meantime, Jeremy had done some revision and reading and then walked the estate with Zulu. He met up with Reverend Paddy and then with Boynton. Both had impressed him. He recognised that achieving close bonds would be prudent. They both struck him as sincere and genuine. Boynton came across as very protective of the Spelthorpe Company, their sons and daughters. Perceptive and knowing, he asked about Jeremy's intentions towards Joanna as it was clear he did not want the girl to get hurt. Jeremy reassured him. He intimated that there were plans afoot but was constrained by agreements and confidence. These plans would not be made public until the summer when both had competed their studies. They took a shot of Jameson's together. Boynton offered to spend a day with him to brief him in greater detail about his work and to reveal parts of the estate that had been missed on cursory inspection. Jeremy took him up on that. He revealed that when lambing started Joanna would be working to gain experience with Ash and that would present an ideal opportunity to take up the offer.

20

Days

January – August 1933.

Lent term commenced on Monday the ninth of January 1933. Jeremy went back to his room at the veterinary school but returned every Saturday to be with Joanna. Both were working hard and when Julia arrived at school to collect the girls for the half term exeat, the housemistress commented on the transformation she had noticed in Joanna. Already it was of note that she was a hard worker but over the last few weeks her performance had risen beyond the scale, whilst at the same time she seemed to be displaying a deep inner happiness that had not previously manifested itself. She asked if Julia had any idea what was behind it. Julia smiled inwardly but bit her lip and said she had no idea.

The shooting season had ended by February, and this was the time that the first lambs had started to arrive. Ash took Joanna in tow. Whilst the shepherds continued with managing and feeding the flock, lambing was Ash's province because of the way he managed the process. Much of this had been drawn from his Medical Corps experience. All sheep that were expected to deliver over the next few days were corralled so they could be watched over. Absolute cleanliness was vital to prevent infection, and this included a disinfectant foot bath at entry and exit points with regular use of clean straw to cover urine and faeces. Observation was critical. Sheep that turned in circles and kicked up the straw to make a nest presented a clue. Regular checking of the rear ends was essential. Most births proceeded naturally with minimal intervention, but if there were delays and indications of distress this meant getting the sheep to the ground and the insertion of a lubricated hand. The front forelegs had to be lined up with the nose and normally a pull on the forelegs would result in delivery but if difficult a lambing rope would be applied to the forelegs. If it was a breech birth and there were no means of quick correction, then a rapid intervention was the rule to get the lamb out. On delivery a piece of straw in the nostril would set off a sneezing reaction to get it breathing, but if not, swinging the lamb and massage usually did the trick. Ash insisted that all lambs had the umbilical cord dipped in an iodine solution.

After birth the sheep and lambs were penned individually, and a watch was maintained. Sometimes a mother would reject her offspring but an appearance by one of the merdogs would normally prompt a protective reaction to replace rejection. If feeding took place naturally that was good but if not, teats were checked. The first milk was much thicker and termed colostrum. This contained the essential antibodies. Ash would draw this off by hand then tube feed it into the lamb's stomach to get things going. Vigilance was the key but despite this there were always cases where things did not go well. Orphaned lambs were kept together and fed by hand from surplus milk. The merdogs would lie in the orphan pens with the lambs all over them until required for a specific task. Mothers with triplets meant one lamb was removed because rarely would the mother sheep be able to feed all three. The lamb would be smeared with fluids from a single newborn or a still born and then introduced to the mother. This trick usually worked. Occasionally a lamb was born with a deformed leg. Ash would splint these up and often in a week or two, normality returned.

Lisette would sometimes help along with the twins. Ash wanted as many as possible to learn about lambing but was conscious that if too many got involved at the same time, communication would break down. But there was a backup. Every pen had a slate with timings and notes in chalk. Joanna learnt quickly but the days were long, and the sight of the two of them covered in straw, muck and blood at three in the morning might not have been endearing to genteel urban folks who wanted their roast lamb on Sundays.

Only when Ash was certain, would the sheep and lambs be released outside, but they could be brought back under cover if night temperatures fell excessively. Jeremy would visit too, conscious of the fact that veterinary theory and working practice did not always go hand in hand, but both he and Joanna could learn from this. A couple of weeks later, Joanna was invited to conduct the castration of male lambs using rubber rings. These were applied to the scrotal sack using a metal tong ring stretcher. Ash, Joanna and Jeremy worked on this as a team. Ash said to Jeremy. "If you see Joanna with this in the bedroom you will know you have upset her. So don't say you have not been warned!"

On other farms this level of care was lacking. Some might mock, but the lamb production and survival rate at Spelthorpe was the best in the county. All that extra work and time bore dividends.

The days went by. At the end of March, the surgery and two houses were completed. The four-bedroom house with garage for the head vet was fifty yards from the surgery. Rufus and his wife Anna took up residence. The surgery was designed with the future in mind with adequate parking, a secure rear yard and pen for livestock, an operating room, laundry room, two consulting rooms, a waiting room and an office with a front counter. There were internal cages and kennels. The house for the second vet was a hundred yards further along directly opposite the church. This had three bedrooms, a large garage and spacious garden. After stocking and any final touches Rufus anticipated that the surgery would open to the public in the summer, but he commenced work on the estate immediately. Anna had agreed to run the office. Jeremy continued to stay at the annex when he visited so as not to encourage any idle talk.

Rufus' salary was fixed from the outset. The formula on the estate was that pay was pinned to military pay levels. Thus, Julian

Johnson with overall charge was paid as a lieutenant colonel. Ash and Rufus were paid as majors. Those running specific areas like Boynton and the harbour master were paid as captains. Foremen were ranked as warrant officers and other tradesmen and farm workers were graded according to their skill levels with apprentices paid as privates. It was a formula that Simon had devised years ago, and it survived because workers regarded it as essentially fair. It stopped any bickering and for many, there were considerable fringe benefits.

The school summer term came to an end in mid-July. Jeremy had come through his final examinations with flying colours and swiftly registered himself as a member of the Royal College of Veterinary Surgeons. The surgery had opened, and he started working there on the equivalent of captain's pay. Joanna had gained top grades and had been accepted at the Cambridge Veterinary School.

Jeremy attended at the school with Julian and Julia on the last day for the final assembly to which parents and relatives were invited. There was the woman he loved walking around in her school uniform. The secret had been preserved, and he couldn't resist an inner giggle. The traditional hymn of '*Lord Dismiss Us with Thy Blessing*' was played, and due to the collective delight of the pupils at the end of term it was sung with a volume and gusto that exceeded any other.

After the assembly the pupils scheduled to return in September took their leave. There was a reception for school leavers and their families. Some of the leavers, including Joanna, had changed into going-home clothes. Most would be going on to university with others departing for officer training in the military. Jeremy had come equipped, and Joanna took the ring and placed it on her finger. They gave each other a little hug and then mingled with the others along with Julia and Julian. Joanna introduced Jeremy to her house mistress who got the wrong end of the stick "And what does your brother do?" she asked.

"He's a veterinary surgeon, but he's not my brother. Jeremy is my fiancé." She displayed her left hand.

The house mistress was somewhat dumbfounded but responded. "My heartfelt congratulations to you both. I asked your mother earlier in the year why you were working so incredibly hard, and that explains it all, but I must thank you for your extreme discretion on the issue. That showed great loyalty to the school."

Joanna replied. "Thank you, miss. I must say that I have enjoyed every day here. You have all been so kind to me, but I discovered that life has a pace of its own and that means at times you have to seize the moment and not lose the opportunity so that's what Jeremy and I did."

"I suppose this means a long engagement," said the housemistress.

"If you call a month a long time," said Joanna. "I know my parents may not be aware, but the vicar is ready and waiting for our call, and we intend to move forward. I know I'm off to Cambridge but it's the veterinary school where Jeremy studied. I will be home at weekends and holidays and for surgery placements at the Spelthorpe veterinary surgery. My husband will be able to call at any time because, as a married woman, that will give me a special status."

"Well, Joanna, you have done your homework, but I'd expect nothing else from you. You always stood out as the most determined scholar I've ever had the pleasure to teach. God bless you both and do come back and see us. We would like that!" With that she shook hands with them both and then with Joanna's parents who were standing behind displaying a mixture of pride and astonishment. Joanna then took off to say goodbye to her close friends. She was keen to show off her man and to put them on notice of an imminent wedding invitation. For Jeremy and Joanna, it was public now and their joy could not be hidden.

On return to Spelthorpe they knew that the news would bounce around the estate at the speed of light. Julian and Julia had been taken off guard by the decision to proceed to marriage so quickly but could understand the rationale behind that. The first thing that Joanna and Julian did was to speak to Reverend Paddy. As the car passed the church, they spotted him cutting the grass in the churchyard, so they jumped out and bounced up to him. He looked up and said, "I know what you want. The Lord has told me, so just name the day and I'll be there for you."

Jeremy answered, "We were thinking about Saturday the twenty-sixth of August as that will give us time to read out the banns and time afterwards for a short honeymoon before Joanna starts at Cambridge."

"Well, I'm delighted for you both and so is the Lord because he told me you were coming, but now I expect you want to go and talk to some people on the estate before they all get gossiping."

They called on Rufus and Anna to deliver the news. "That's brilliant said Rufus, because that new house opposite the church needs an occupier and now you are official that will stop any tongues wagging."

They expressed their delight at the news.

The next stop was Simon and Helen who were equally astonished at their pace and determination. Simon said. "Pace and determination but that's the Spelthorpe way and we are proud of you both. Our present to you will be the reception here in the Hall so you won't have to worry about that. The estate will cover it. The large dining room will easily take a hundred guests with a bit of furniture moving. Amrik and his team will sort that out."

They moved on and drove up to see Boynton. Jeremy said. "I've got quite close to Boynton. He cares about you a lot. So,

I think we should invite him to the wedding and reception but although it might be hilarious, I cannot have him as best man. Can you imagine his speech if he resorts to his male-only language? It would be totally sincere and memorable but sometimes we have to do what is expected. Ash will be the best man, but I haven't asked him yet."

Joanna had an attack of the giggles when she thought of Boynton's speech but agreed. "He's a bit of a ruffian at times, but he's a thoroughly decent man and I want him there. A lot of the ladies on the estate like him."

Boynton was overcome when they told him and said they wanted him to come to the wedding and reception. He was delighted to be one of the first to know. Any uncertainty that he previously held concerning them, was now over.

On the next day once the shock had sunk in, Julian hosted a party in the annexe for the Spelthorpe Company, along with Rufus and Anna. Ash had agreed to act as the best man. Jennifer, Victoria and Lucy were recruited as the bridesmaids. All that remained to set in motion was for Joanna to head off to Norwich alongside her mother, Helen and Lisette to deal with dress issues. For Joanna and Jeremy there was joy that their engagement was now out in the open but there was something of an anti-climax in that they missed the frisson that came with the secrecy. The number of guests would not be excessive. Both wanted three or four close friends each. From the estate, it would be limited to Rev Paddy and Ruth and Boynton. Joanna additionally wanted to invite her housemistress from the school and the two grooms from the stable who had always treated her with kindness and consideration. With a few others suggested by parents of the bride and groom that made for about fifty in all. Essentially both bride and groom wanted it to remain low-key with close family and treasured friends.

The actual wedding would be open to all, but Joanna insisted that the merdogs attend inside along with Zulu and Gelert, and her two favourite horses should be tethered outside the church.

The next month was spent in preparation for the new home, but time was always allocated for rides along the sands and in the surf. Ash had persuaded them both to take up the wild swimming. It was not something that Joanna had done to any great extent but both she and Jeremy caught the bug and combined it with bareback riding into the waves with the merdogs charging along at the side.

The big day finally arrived. It was a splendid affair but what made it different was the genuine goodwill and affection shown by the guests not just to the bride and groom but to each other. Reverend Paddy reminded all that Christ's first miracle was at the wedding at Cana. The meeting of Joanna and Jeremy should go down as the first miracle at Spelthorpe. Although on this occasion, Reverend Paddy may not be able to convert the water into wine. Nevertheless, he said he was working on it.

Boynton felt especially honoured and somehow, he worked his charms on Joanna's former housemistress. It was in a sense of mischief that Joanna had made sure they sat next to one another. They enjoyed their drinks, and rumours later abounded that he took her home with him at the end of the day.

On the following day Mr and Mrs Jeremy de Lisle left for a five-day honeymoon in the Lake District.

21

1937

Days turned into months and months turned into years. The pattern of the seasons and work on the estate had carried on as before. The three families worked hard but played hard too and recognised their good fortune to experience nature first-hand. They saw the new seals in the spring and marvelled at the vibrant greens on the trees in the deer park. In the autumn, there would be a kaleidoscope of colour as varieties of leaves turned to golds, yellows and reds. These produced treasure in the early morning mists across the valley bottoms.

In the summer of 1936 Joanna had graduated from the veterinary school and was now registered. She specialised in small animal work because that's what the expanding surgery needed, but she maintained capability across the board. Her sister Jennifer was halfway into her medical training at Cambridge.

Michael and Victoria had taken to horse riding often with the merdogs alongside. They were both approaching seventeen years and their mutual affection continued unabated. On one such ride in late November of the previous year Nimrod had suddenly taken off on a scent. They found him ten minutes later tied with Tan, Boynton's bitch. In early February a litter of six arrived. Ash, looking ahead as ever, and mindful of succession planning, took a dog who he named Shackleton after the famous explorer. Joanna and Jeremy took a bitch who they called Boudicca or Boudi for short.

The twins continued with the annual pilgrimage to France to see the grandparents. They were now of sufficient age to go and return unaccompanied. Lucy was happy to go but with a limited holiday period Michael did not want to leave Victoria and for this year had managed to persuade his mother to allow Victoria to go with them on the basis that it would improve her French. The earl was supportive. At least Michael now knew the English meaning of 'un capote anglaise'. Boynton who never missed anything had noticed that the pair were making increased visits to the castle. Protective as ever, he approached Michael. "I know what you are up to son," he said. "But don't you be a putting that lovely lass of yours in the pudding club or else the earl will have your guts for garters." He then gave him a handful of condoms and told him how he could get more. Michael's short hair was very noticeable for the rest of the summer.

The merdogs had continued to meet with Minerva on a regular basis taking occasional trips over the years. They had encountered the Vikings when they raided Lindisfarne. On another occasion they encountered William the Bastard as he was known when he stumbled and fell on the beach as he landed with his Norman invaders at Pevensey in 1066. Those with him thought it a bad omen but he grasped to handfuls of sand and tuned bad luck into good by saying that he had seized England in his hands. On another trip they met iguanas, frigate birds, giant tortoises and blue footed boobies – birds that reminded them of the blue-balled vervet monkeys in Kenya, and there was a man from a ship named after a dog who said his name was Darwin.

The cottage by the sea had been transformed with gas and running water with hot baths on offer but the Spelthorpe hillbillies continued to bathe in the sea and the lake because that was what they were used to, and the young Victoria had adopted their outdoor habits. Helen never seemed to mind saying that Eau de Spelthorpe was cheaper than Eau de Cologne. Victoria, Lucy and Michael were all competent drivers because since the age of fourteen they had been driving cars, tractors and the truck on the estate roads. This was the established pattern. The actual driving test remained a mere formality when age allowed it.

The airfield had been constructed courtesy of the Royal Engineers, who did it as a training exercise. Rufus had an old friend who was a colonel in the Engineers. Their levelling and grading equipment was perfect for the job and the estate now boasted two 1000-yard runways. The Engineers received a generous boost to their benevolent fund.

There was now a hangar that could accommodate three aircraft together with a building for conferences and dining. The estate had its own Tiger Moth and Gipsy Moth planes and Simon now took on a part-time instructor – a veteran ace of the Royal Flying Corps who had flown with top ace James McCudden in the war. Young Michael had been up with Simon and as the planes had dual controls, he was fast becoming a competent flyer. He was yet to go solo. Simon had arranged for extra tuition with the instructor.

Financially the estate was in good health. The national depression was starting to ebb. The veterinary practice had saved a small fortune and was profitable in its own right, but importantly it was providing a valuable service to the nearby villages and other farms. For the huge efforts made by Rufus and Jeremy to get things off the ground bonuses had been paid. The work continued to increase. Joanna's graduation had come at the right time, and she too was now getting the equivalent of a captain's salary.

Geoffrey de Havilland had been back to demonstrate his latest Dragon Rapide twin-engine plane that could take up to eight passengers at 150 mph for some 500 miles. Some of the shooting parties were now arriving in this aircraft. It attracted visitors from further afield and the fact that they could get there, shoot, dine, shoot again and get back still in daylight added to the appeal. All the other planned work with the roads, tracks and utility connections had now been completed, along with ten luxury cabins on the east side of the coastal lake.

In respect of the Sandringham connection, as foreseen, the wheel did come off. King George died in January of 1936 and 'David' succeeded him as expected. He chose the name Edward VIII as his regal name, but it was then that his playboy lifestyle caught up with him. Both the establishment at home and in the overseas dominions were not going to have an American double divorcee as their future queen. Any requirement to marry a virgin had been discontinued in the Middle Ages, but Edward's insistence of marriage was just not on. It would be like wearing a suit that had been through two second-hand shops and for an English monarch that was totally unacceptable. Bertie had taken Simon into his confidence on this and the telephone line between Spelthorpe and Sandringham had been well used. Over the years the relationship had matured. What Bertie cared about most of all was his immediate family. He shunned crowds but did his royal duty as and when required, all despite his stammer which was aggravated when he was not at ease. Joanna and Julian made periodic visits because Lillibet loved to see them. Major Rufus had been taken into the fold as Bertie valued his extensive horse expertise. As a former military man holding the King's Commission he was trusted.

What finally transpired was what Bertie dreaded with Edward's abdication in December. In an instant Bertie had the greatness that he never wanted thrust upon him. To make matters worse, having ditched the monarchy, Edward kept the personal spoils that he had inherited from his father and the new king had to buy back both Sandringham and Balmoral. This made any reconciliation highly unlikely.

As a high-ranking members of the peerage Simon and Helen were invited to the coronation on Wednesday 12th May 1937 but the king insisted that all adult members of the triumvirate including the de Lisles attend as guests. The new king maintained contact, but visits were fewer owing to the exigencies of his new role.

The twelfth of May presented an opportunity for the merdogs. Michael and Lucy were at school. The merdogs sought out Minerva on the beach and introduced Shackleton as the newest member of the pack. He was just over twelve weeks old but was instantly taken on board as a full member. Ash had left it to them to train him. Long walks with Shackleton were out of the question. Minerva met them opposite the gap. She told Shackleton what to expect but before becoming a merdog he would have to grow a bit and become a competent swimmer, but the other dogs would see to that in the year ahead.

Minerva asked if Kipling and Nimrod could meet her at the pool in an hour's time. The others took Shackleton back the cottage. Kipling and Nimrod took a walk up to the pool examining what the tide had washed up.

They got to the pool where Minerva was waiting so they dived in and disappeared below the surface. On coming up things were similar but different. There were dunes and a sandy beach with pines. In the distance, behind the dunes was a large, tented camp and a similar smaller camp to the right of them.

A party of boys all in uniform were marching along the beach. They were all carrying spades like a soldier would carry a rifle, and they were singing in unison. They wore shorts and brown shirts, and all had a strange black cross badge with feet sticking out at the ends. The boys started digging in a line and there were men with them in uniform too. From the smaller camp three teenage girls emerged with a young woman. They had white shirts with black ties and black shorts. They were all blondes and had the same black cross symbol on their uniform. They had an Alsatian dog with them. It was on a lead.

"Is that a dog or a bitch?" asked Kipling.

"It's a bitch," said Nimrod. "I'm an expert on bitches."

"And don't we all know it," said Kipling. "That's how we ended up with Shackleton. Tell me, Minerva, where are we?"

"This is Northern Germany on the Baltic Coast and these are two camps. The large camp is for the Hitler Youth. They are like Boy Scouts, but they are very military. All boys apart from Jews, must belong to the Hitler Youth. It's the law. These people are Nazis, and they say they want to kill all the Jews because they blame them and the communists for losing the war. They keep beating them up and locking them up. The girls are from the League of German girls. They are like the Hitler Youth but they are training to be wives and mothers and to make babies who will be soldiers."

The girls with the dog approached. Kip and Nimrod wagged their tails, and the woman said, "You can let Blonda off. These dogs look friendly, and I think Blonda wants to play. She will come back when I call her."

"Are you sure Fraulein Braun?" asked one of the girls.

"That's right. I spend a lot of time with the Fuhrer and Blonda. If you can pose with Blonda and the dogs, I will take some photos. I'm sure that the Fuhrer will like that. He loves dogs," said Fraulein Braun.

"And we all love the Fuhrer," said one of the girls. "And it is wonderful that he is visiting our camp. I shook his hand. It was electrifying. It was the most wonderful thing that has ever happened to me."

Blonda joined the dogs, and they played on the edge of the sea. They introduced themselves. Blonda explained things: "I am Hitler's dog. They all think he is the man who saved Germany. He says that I am the only one he trusts because he breaks out into rages and screams at people. They are terrified of him and all the time he keeps saying how he hates the Jews and how he is going to get rid of them. He's very strange because he thinks all Germans should have blonde hair and blue eyes. Most of the girls here are like that because they will make the best mothers when they marry and have sons who will make the best German soldiers. I think he wants to breed people like some people breed dogs, so they all look the same. Next, they will get rid of the mongrels, but I've met some nice mongrels. Deep down I don't think he likes dogs. He just does it to be popular with people. He does the same with children, but I'll just have to make the most of it. Better than being a mongrel I suppose, and I do get fed and Eva, that's Fraulein Braun, she is most kind to me. He had a niece as a girlfriend before Eva. He wasn't nice to her, and she shot herself with his gun. He doesn't like people to know about that. And as for all this blonde hair and blue eyes, none of the people close to Hitler look like that. They are all a bit odd, if you want the truth, and most of them would not make good soldiers anyway."

Eva got the dogs to all pose with the girls for a few photos. All the girls raised their arms high and shouted 'Heil Hitler' as the photo was taken.

The boys further along the beach heard the shout and they all raised their arms and shouted the same.

After the photo Eva put Blonda back on the lead, and they started to go back to the camp.

"This is all very strange," said Nimrod. "Are all Germans like this?"

Minerva responded. "They are now. They never used to be like it, and they could think for themselves and say what they wanted but not anymore. Hitler just kept getting more and more popular, but that was because he just got gangs of men in brown shirts to beat up and kill people who were against him. In the end enough people were stupid enough to vote for him, and then he changed the law to give him absolute power, so everyone is terrified of a knock on the door in the night because there are spies everywhere telling tales. People just keep quiet and don't say anything and when people are beaten up, they don't help them either. Those boys are practising digging trenches for war. That's all they do. It's as if they want to train everyone for war."

"I don't like this place or the people. It's like they are all hypnotised. They are making them into robots, and killer ones at that who can't think for themselves," said Kipling.

They looked up. About fifty yards away they saw a shortish man with a small moustache wearing a brown blazer and officer cap. He had a red armband with the same black-cross symbol. Soldiers with guns and men in leather coats were close to him.

He greeted the girls and patted the dog, and they saluted him in the same way with arms raised.

"Now you have seen him it's time to get out of here – in case he thinks you are mongrels!" said Minerva. And with that they swam out and dived beneath the waves.

Seconds later they surfaced at the pool.

Nimrod said, "You've taken us to lots of places Minerva but that's the only one I feel bad about. There's something very evil going on there. I'm so glad we are back. We are all happy here because most dogs and people are kind."

Minerva responded, "Yes, you are right, but I thought you should know what is going on. You and your family and their friends are all good, kind people, and when I see that and what is going on in Germany, I worry for them and the future!"

Nonetheless, the dogs thanked Minerva for the visit and told her they would tell the other members of the pack.

22

Our hope for years to come

Midsummer had arrived. It was a Monday on a school exeat weekend. Edward and George would not be heading back until Tuesday evening, so a family gathering was planned for later in the day. Jeremy and Joanna had risen early and walked the short distance down to the new road that ran parallel to the inlet so they could see the sunrise over Seal Island. Boudicca was with them. She was only allowed on short walks because as vets, both were only too aware that over-exercise of growing dogs could result in skeletal problems.

As they left the cottage a car drove by. The female driver looked away as she drove past. "My God," exclaimed Joanna. "That was my old housemistress, Miss Featherstone. We always thought she was so prim and proper, a confirmed spinster but I suppose it's nice to see she has another side. She's kept that quiet. She must be in her early forties now."

"And clearly a regular addition to Boynton's harem. He's a dark horse that Boynton," said Jeremy.

"What do you mean harem?" asked Joanna.

"So, you didn't know," said Jeremy. "Ash told me. His father lives in one of the estate houses and he's spotted Boynton in the darkness visiting the homes of some of the war widows. He's been doing it for years, but he keeps them all happy, so we keep quiet about it". They watched the sunrise then walked back and took a stroll around the church opposite. "It's coming up to four years since we were married here," said Jeremy. "And winter is on its way again."

"That never worries me," said Joanna. "The seasons give us variety and we can all share in that with those we love." She clenched his hand. "After the morning surgery I thought I'd take one of the horses out for a ride and go and see Lisette, but I won't be able to do that for much longer."

"Why's that? Are you going off horses?" asked Jeremy.

She looked into his eyes. "I'd never do that. It is simply that sometime in December we will be three. I've had it confirmed because I wanted to be sure before I told you."

Jeremy was speechless. He kissed her and held her then said "I wondered why the sudden urge to visit Lisette when you will see her at the end of the day. Have you told my father?"

She looked puzzled. "I thought I'd tell the father before the grandfather. What made you say that?"

"They say that pregnancy can induce forgetfulness in women, but we have to keep you away from livestock, particularly the sheep and cattle when they are calving. I thought you would have remembered that. There is a small risk of cross infection. We must review our procedures for washing dirty clothing as well. I know it's only a small risk but I'm not taking any chances. From now on you stick to dogs, cats, tortoises and guinea pigs."

"Yes, I did forget. I'm sorry, but I've had no exposure, and I did no lambing this year because Michael, Lucy and Victoria were learning and helping out." she responded.

"Have you thought of any names yet?" asked Jeremy and he continued, "I suppose it will have to start with a "J" as that is the family tradition. I did think about this ages ago."

"Well, I know he or she is coming at Christmas, and I know Revered Paddy said that our coming together was the first miracle of Spelthorpe ordained from on high, but it's not going to be Jesus if that's what you were thinking." said Joanna.

"No, I wouldn't force that on you. I was thinking of James for a boy and Juliet for a girl but if it's a girl and the next one's a boy he won't be a Romeo. That would be torture for them when they went to school."

They returned home had breakfast. At 8 am they went to the surgery taking Boudicca with them who had become the surgery dog. Rufus and Anna were already there. Both were thrilled by the news and Rufus undertook to implement a new regime until the risk was abated. They agreed with their son's request to keep things on a need-to-know basis until the visual indications would make that impossible. The actual surgery worked on a morning-only basis and that would continue with Joanna taking the lead for the next few months whilst Rufus and Jeremy would do all the agricultural business and callouts.

Midsummer's day was to be memorable for Michael. He had been taking his flying lessons seriously. At 9 am he took a flight with Simon who merely sat there for the whole flight. He did the same half an hour later with the instructor who confirmed Simon's view that he was ready. An audience had gathered and then at 10 am Michael went off on his own in the Gipsy Moth displaying all the overconfidence of youth. He made several circuits, take-offs and landings, and then he took the plane up to 2,000 feet and climbed further and more steeply to produce a stall, which he corrected with perfection. He dived down and made a low-level pass in front of the audience then climbed higher to give a greater margin for error and made another pass with a victory roll, something he had done before, but it was not part of the set routine.

He landed and was greeted by Simon and the instructor who were not happy about the breach of procedure. "Young man!" said the instructor. "There are old pilots and bold pilots, but there are no old bold pilots." Michael swiftly apologised. Then the instructor added, "Well done Biggles…but remember what I said. I will take you further, but you stick to my rules!"

"Thank you, sir," said Michael and he ran across to Victoria who was waiting on the edge of the runway. She gave him a huge hug.

The instructor turned to Simon and Ash. "The boy's got balls. He will do well but a few words of caution will not go amiss at this stage. I've always found that lads like Michael who are prepared to take things further on their own initiative are the one's that excel. They make the fighter pilots of the future. The rest are good pilots but better suited to other types of planes. Michael is a natural flyer, and I see hints of a killer instinct there. I can help with that if you want him to go that way but for now let him enjoy the moment and, if and when he is ready for more, I will be there for you. What does he want to do?"

Ash said. "He's not sure at the moment. He keeps debating with himself over the navy or the air force. He's a good sailor, good on the water too, and he swims like a fish but it's still early days. He won't finish school until after another full school year so we shall see."

After surgery Joanna rode up to see Lisette and to give her the news, so they had plenty to talk about as they prepared for the afternoon event. The tide would be at its height at 4 pm. 'Biggles' received full congratulations when Joanna heard the news.

The party took off at 3 pm. All the members of the three families and the de Lisles were there along with all the dogs and two of the ponies. Even Jennifer had managed to get away as she had no lectures or practicals for that day. The weather was perfect with just a slight breeze. The heat on the mud flats had warmed the water as the tide came in.

Everyone took a swim. Bareback riding in the surf had become the new local fashion and most of the younger members took part with Joanna taking something of a lead.

Tables and chairs had been laid out on a flat area closer to the dunes. At 6pm there was a mouth-watering display of chicken and sausages, with jacket potatoes and salads which were devoured as the sun steadily got lower in the western sky and the tide receded.

Drinks were served on a help-yourself basis and the families gravitated into three groups with Simon, Ash, JJ, Jeremy and Rufus discussing the state of the world. The ladies including Joanna and Jennifer talked at a distance and then the younger members were playing rounders on the mud flats with the dogs fielding.

A monoplane came flying along the coastline at great speed. The engine let out a throaty roar that oozed sheer power. It passed them by then did a roll and a loop, then turned and flew past them again. "That's the new Hawker Hurricane, our latest fighter," said Simon. "The king told me that they have just ordered 600 of them and there's another faster one going through its trials, but I don't know the name for that one. They both have eight machine guns and go well over 300 mph."

Ash came in. "And not before time with all this going on in Germany with that crazy Bohemian corporal running the show. Have you seen him at the cinema with his speeches? The whole population has been brainwashed. Three months ago, they went back into the Rhineland, and we did nothing. The French did nothing, and you can't rely on them. They spend all their time fighting amongst themselves. They keep changing governments and now we have got that Oswald Mosely, the fascist rabble rouser doing a copycat over here. The Germans are not supposed to have an air force, but they flattened that place in northern Spain a couple of months back. Killed hundreds."

"Guernica," said Simon. "That was the name of the place and from what the king tells me, his brother is in league with them. Apparently, he and that woman have been invited to do a tour over there. No one in government is best pleased with that, as you can imagine."

Rufus added. "Well, it seems from what you say that at long last someone in government is waking up. They've all had their heads in the sand for the last four years and the only one taking the threat seriously is, Winston Churchill. But they all dismissed him as 'Winnie the warmonger' and left him out in the cold."

JJ said, "I've been worried and increasingly so. We had our war – the war to end wars, as they called it, but all we have had for the last eighteen years is half-time before the next one. Half-time to bury the dead, time to build memorials and time to raise a new crop of young men to go to the slaughter, and it won't be just young men next time. I know they killed a few nurses in the last one. When Guernica happened, it dawned on me that they couldn't care less who they killed: men, women and children. In the next war I tell you it will be ordinary people and not just soldiers who will bear the brunt of it. They will bomb us and without fighter aircraft in large numbers that will be it. It's all right having the biggest navy in the world, but battleships can't shoot down bombers high in the sky. We know that from the Zeppelin and the Gotha raids in the last war that they never stick to the rules. There is something really evil in the German psyche that allows them to think that is all right."

They recharged their glasses, and the women joined them as the sun gradually went down behind the castle. Lisette had picked up their conversation.

"I know it's gloomy thing you have been talking about but look out there where the children are playing. We have all been happy today and life has been kind. Whatever comes our way, we will get through it as we did in the past. I can see Paddy out there with Ruth shrimping. He will help guide us, but most of all we have each other and the love we share will see us all through."

"I'll second that," said Simon "Look at those dogs on the edge of the sea in a semi-circle! They are all there. It looks like they are talking with somebody."

"That's the merdogs," said Lisette. "And they are with their mermaid, but we shall all keep that as our secret. I suppose, one day, someone might even write a book about it."

They raised their glasses and hugged one another, as the sun finally set behind the castle.

The end

…to be continued in the sequel *Spelthorpe at War*

About the Author

**The author swimming with three of the original merdogs:
Trooper, Rafe and Hunter**

Ashley Clark spent thirty years with the Kent County Constabulary. In his early service at the age of twenty years he was probably the youngest village constable in England when he looked after several villages around Betteshanger near Deal, Kent. The bulk of his service was spent as a detective. For his last 12 years, for much of the time he was based in France where he worked closely with French counterparts from the Police Nationale and the Gendarmerie. On retiring from the police, he worked as a schools' battlefield guide for some fifteen years taking both school and adult groups to the battlefields of France and Belgium. At the same time, he intermittently occupied himself on a Kent sheep farm and a large Exmoor shooting estate. He is widely travelled and lives in Whitstable, Kent where for the last twenty years has led the group that manages and maintains an award-winning nature reserve – believed to be the largest village green in England. In the warmer months he swims daily in the sea with his Labradors.

Historic note

Some of the chapters and terminology may require a little further explanation:

Chapter 3
The Sandringham Company under Captain Beck was real. They served in Gallipoli in 1915 and disappeared as they went forward in an engagement. Subsequently after the war a number of bodies were found but the precise manner of the deaths remains disputed. The BBC drama 'All the King's Men" tells the story.

The invasion of neutral Belgium was the justification for Britain to declare war. During the invasion many Belgian civilians were murdered by the invaders. At Dinant and Leuven several hundred civilians were killed.

The British army placed great priority on what they referred to as musketry (Rifle skills in respect of accuracy and speed). When the British Expeditionary Force (BEF) met up with the Germans at Mons where they were outnumbered by four to one. British fire was so accurate that it took a heavy toll on the enemy who were of the view that the BEF were equipped with large numbers of machine guns.

A jam tin bomb was a simple hand grenade made with an old jam tin stuffed with metal debris and explosives with a lit fuse. They were unreliable and replaced at the end of 1915 with the Mills bomb which had a safety pin. The author's great uncle lost an eye in 1915 when he threw a jam-tin bomb. It was caught by a German who threw it back.

The sinking of the Lusitania off the coast of Ireland resulted in the loss of over a thousand civilian lives many of whom were Americans. Controversy remains as the liner was believed to be carrying munitions.

The Aubers Ridge battle is described factually throughout other than the attachment of the Spelthorpians. The action is described in the official war diary of the first battalion of the Northamptonshire Regiment. The Northampton Regiment private, Harry, who went over in the first wave and had lost his brother Fred earlier were the grandfather and great uncle of the author.

The casualty figures are accurate (other than those of the Spelthorpians). The mention of Wadhurst in Sussex is genuine with 25 deaths including two sets of brothers. The author has taken the pupils of the Wadhurst's Uplands Academy to the battlefield on several occasions.

The battle of Aubers Ridge is significant in that it led to the shell crisis that ultimately resulted in the sidelining of Field Marshall Kitchener as the Secretary of State for War. Field Marshall Sir John French was replaced by Field Marshall Douglas Haig. In 1916 Prime Minister Herbert Asquith was replaced by David Lloyd- George.

Blighty is a word in one of the Indian languages that the British soldier adopted to mean home. Thus a "Blighty" wound was one that got one out of the conflict and back home.

Chapter 4
The portrait and events at Folkestone including the Gotha Raid are entirely accurate and part of the description has been taken from eyewitness accounts. Folkestone was the main port used to take soldiers to France. The wounded normally returned via Dover, so they were not seen by departing troops. More information is available at the Folkestone Museum, 'Dover and Folkestone during the Great War' by Michael and Christine George and 'Folkestone in the war {1914-1919} a record of town's life and work' compiled by John Carlile.

Chapter 8
The bombing of the Etaples hospital complex took place several times in May 1918 and the victims are buried in the Etaples Military Cemetery managed by the Commonwealth War Graves Commission. This is the largest British cemetery in France. The war diary of the Base Commandant tells us that 169 were killed on 19th May 1918. (National Archives reference WO95/4027)

Chapter 9
The meeting with the young Nelson is fictional but the background material is accurate.

Five shillings was the pre-decimal equivalent of twenty-five pence (Twenty-two pounds at today's prices)

TE Lawrence (Lawrence of Arabia) was not always alone in his war with the Arabs against the Turks. A number of British soldiers also participated in his raids.

Chapter 12

William Clark was one of the great-uncles of the author. He died of gas poisoning and is buried in the Etaples cemetery.

The incredible story of Jackie- the war baboon, and his treatment after injury is entirely true. After the war he raised money for the Red Cross and then returned to South Africa where he he died in 1921.

VAD means Voluntary Aid Detachment. The soldiers sometimes referred to them as 'Very Adorable Darlings' Their numbers included crime writer Agatha Christie and the author and peace campaigner Vera Brittain (author of Testament of Youth).

ANZAC – a member of the Australian and New Zealand Army Corps

Chapter 13

The Billy Butlin camp at Skegness was his first. It was opened in 1936. Others followed.

Munitionettes were female munitions factory workers. They were highly paid by the standards of the day. The work was dangerous.

Chapter 14

A 'priest' is the name given to a lump of dense wood to administer the last rites to a wounded bird or fish.

Chapter 15

The man-eaters of Tsavo were a serious problem when building the railway that stretched from Mombasa on the coast to Uganda. The railway made development possible further inland. Large numbers of workers were brought across from the Indian subcontinent. Many stayed in Africa but were expelled from Uganda in the 1970s under Idi Amin.

Chapter 16

The castle keep does not exist along the north Norfolk coastline, but it is inspired by the splendid keep on the Suffolk coast at Orford. There is a local legend of a merman.

The Kaiser who abdicated in 1918, fled to the Netherlands in 1918 where he remained in exile until his death in 1941. The Dutch exported large amounts of foodstuffs to Germany in the Great War. At the time food was in short supply in Germany due to the British Naval blockade.

Chapter 18

Knowlton in Kent was dubbed the 'bravest village' following a campaign in 1915 by the Weekly Dispatch publication due to its claim to have the largest proportion of villagers to volunteer.

Chapter 21

Capote anglaise – Old french slang for a condom – English bonnet. At the same time, the English referred to them as French letters.

Blonda – Hitler had two female dogs both called Blonda. These were German Shepherds. The English renamed these dogs as Alsatians because of an intense dislike of anything German.

Hitler's more famous dog which he had later was called Blondi. It was a German Shepherd bitch.

Chapter 22

The Duke and Duchess of Windsor (formerly Edward VIII and Mrs Simpson) experienced a ten-day tour of Nazi Germany in October 1937 where they met Hitler.